NEWTON
and the
TIME
MACHINE

NEWTON
and the
TIME
MACHINE

Michael McGowan
Illustrated by Shelagh McNulty

HarperTrophyCanada™
An imprint of HarperCollinsPublishersLtd

Newton and the Time Machine
Text © 2008 by Michael McGowan.
All rights reserved.

Published by HarperTrophyCanada™,
an imprint of HarperCollins
Publishers Ltd

First edition

HarperCollins books may be pur-
chased for educational, business, or
sales promotional use through our
Special Markets Department.

HarperCollins Publishers Ltd
2 Bloor Street East, 20th Floor
Toronto, Ontario, Canada
M4W 1A8

www.harpercollins.ca

Library and Archives Canada
Cataloguing in Publication

McGowan, Michael, 1966–
Newton and the time machine /
Michael McGowan.

ISBN 978-0-00-639550-8

I. Title.

PS8575.G663N49 2008   JC813´.6
C2008-900866-9

WB 9 8 7 6 5 4 3 2

Newton and the Time Machine is printed on
Ancient Forest Friendly paper, made
with 100% post-consumer waste.

Printed in Canada

For Shelagh, Henry, Wiley and Frances

CHAPTER ONE

Newton was having serious, serious doubts that his latest invention—a time machine—was ready to be field-tested.

"What do you think? Should we start it up?" Max, his best friend, asked.

Newton had been staring at the machine for more than four minutes without moving. "Shh!" Newton put up a finger. Now was not a good time to be answering questions. "I'm trying to concentrate." He coughed loudly, wishing that Herbert would stop licking Queen Gertrude's toes. The slurping made it hard to think. They were the rulers of the Kingdom of the Merriwarts—a peaceful race of giants who lived in trees—and Newton wished they'd behave a tad more . . . royally.

The newlyweds ignored him. To Merriwarts toe-licking was like dogs sniffing each others' butts—completely natural. Slobber was pooling on the floor of his laboratory—a converted Merriwart tree fort.

Newton's head hurt, right in the hollow at the back of his head, a sure sign that he'd overlooked something (unless the pain was caused by a deadly brain tumour). But what? Though Newton was always cautious when it came to testing his inventions, this dread was something altogether different. Maybe he was feeling this way because the time machine was an invention of a significantly greater magnitude. Glitches could have disastrous results. What would happen if the machine only half-worked? Would flesh rip apart during transportation? Would eyeballs explode? Earlobes melt? Would the machine send someone back to a place they could never return from?

Commander Joe, a plastic action figure and also Official Military Consultant (for the role he had played in saving the kingdom), was in the pocket of Newton's lab coat getting antsy. He punched Newton in the chest and barked, "Come on, Pokey! You going soft? Afraid to put it on the line?" Pokey was Commander Joe's nickname for Newton. Joe had been calling him that for forever, even though it still embarrassed Newton.

The punch hurt, but Newton was lost in thought. He had spent countless hours wiring and fusing, spinning electrons and bending time. In his gut, he knew the machine was ready, and yet something was bugging him. Maybe he should have waited a few more days to gather his friends.

What was really bothering him? Was he just nervous? Afraid of failure? He took a deep breath.

"I'm ready," he said, though he felt like he was anything but. "I just have to do one more thing."

"Safety first, people! Let's put on our protective goggles! That's an order!" Commander Joe barked.

"Everything's an order with you," Max grumbled.

Commander Joe hopped out of Newton's pocket, jumped over to Max and twisted his nose. "You got a problem with that, soldier?"

Tears were coming out of Max's eyes. "No," he managed to say. "Take it easy."

"I'll take it easy when discipline is established," Commander Joe warned, and then let go of Max's nose before swinging back over to Newton.

Herbert was still licking Gertrude's feet and the Queen had practically passed out with joy.

"HEY, TWINKLE TOES!" Commander Joe shouted, and both Herbert and Gertrude looked up. "If you two expect to stay and watch the show, put on your goggles ASAP."

Reluctantly the giants did as the tiny toy soldier ordered.

Gertrude whispered to Herbert, "He seems to be taking his role as Military Consultant way too seriously, don't you think?"

Herbert moaned in agreement, then added. "I was about to gnaw at the toe-fungus beside your pinky."

"Don't worry, Herbie," Gertrude cooed. "Just think about how much more my feet will sweat and fester while we're waiting."

A disgusting line of drool slid off Herbert's chin as he anticipated the foot fantasies that might soon be realized.

Newton tried not to pay attention to these distractions as he soldered the wire connecting the photoreceptor to the atomic warper—a difficult operation under ideal circumstances. He had been afraid to finish this critical step any earlier, just in case the machine became unsteady. He was so excited his hands shook. When the connection was properly fused, Newton solemnly said, "It's ready. Maybe we'll finally be able to meet some dinosaurs!"

"And visit Genghis Khan!" Commander Joe added enthusiastically.

"And see the Hanging Gardens of Babylon!" Max declared.

"Sure," Newton replied, glad that his friends were so certain the machine would work, but afraid that he was going to disappoint them severely. "Give me a hand."

Though the time machine was not much bigger than an outhouse, it was heavy. The surface was covered with a thin sheet of tin, with rivets holding it in place. Exhaust pipes snaked out of the domed roof, while dials and pressure gauges dotted the sides. A steel door led into the compression chamber. It took all of Gertrude and Herbert's muscle power to slide the machine out to the deck of the tree fort.

"What's in this thing, Newton?" Herbert panted, after the machine had been positioned.

"Well, a fair bit of lead, which I'm hoping will insulate the fusion reactor and not cause a complete meltdown."

Max put his fingers over his nose. "Speaking of meltdowns, Herbert, all that sweating has made you stink with a capital P-U!" It was true. Newton wouldn't have been surprised to see a noxious green gas hovering around Herbert's armpits.

Herbert blushed as Gertrude hugged him, breathed in deeply and smiled. "If we could bottle the aroma, I have no doubt we'd get rich selling it."

"Come on, Wiggins, stop stalling. Turn on the time machine. I need to be home for dinner," Max urged. "My mom is making cabbage rolls." Max adored cabbage rolls.

"Okay, okay," Newton replied after rechecking everything. This was it. There were no excuses to delay any longer. The moment of truth had arrived. "Everyone might want to stand back—"

"STAND BACK! I REPEAT, STAND BACK!" Commander Joe shouted. Everyone obeyed.

Using a long stick, Newton leaned in and delicately poked at the green start button like a lion tamer prodding an angry animal. Twice he pulled the stick back before the button had been pushed hard enough to kick-start the machine. The third time he pressed harder and the button finally engaged.

Except that nothing happened. Absolutely nothing.

"Is it working?" Gertrude asked.

"I'm not sure," Newton replied. "Hopefully it's performing all the pre—" He didn't have time to finish his sentence because the time machine began whirring and buzzing. Lights came on, illuminating the numbers on the control panel. A swirling mass of dust was moving like a mini-tornado in the transport chamber.

Max turned to Newton. "Well . . . ?"

"So far everything seems to be in order. I think." In fact, everything, right down to the pressure gauges, appeared to be functional.

Newton had always been a curious kid. He needed to know everything, from how the remote control for the television worked to why humans have hair on the tops of their toes. However, nothing quite tickled his curiosity bone like dinosaurs. Newton's was a late-blooming interest brought on by the recent discovery of an intact stegosaurus skeleton on the edge of town last year. As the crack team of archaeologists unearthed the beast's bones, tyrannosaurus, stegosaurus and brachiosaurus had grabbed hold of his imagination.

Over the weeks he had exhaustively researched everything he could about them and become something of an expert chronicling his findings in journals #27 and #28. In fact, Newton could probably match wits with leading palaeontologists, his knowledge was that extensive. You might guess that books, movies and video games would have helped quench Newton's curiosity; however, you would be wrong. In fact, the more information Newton absorbed, the more he wanted to confirm for himself the truth about these creatures. It wasn't as if he didn't believe in their existence, rather, he wanted actual proof that the piles of bones so carefully put back together in museum displays were capable of eating medium-sized trees in a gulp. So much so that number one on his Top Ten Life Goals was to meet a living, breathing dinosaur. However, as everyone already knows, there's one gigantic problem with trying to get up-close and personal with these prehistoric beasts. They're extinct. Kaput. Don't exist any more. Finito. Bye-bye.

But Newton wasn't discouraged by that fact. Instead, he put his considerable brainpower to work, theorizing, calculating and designing a way around this problem until at long last, he came up with a solution: a time machine. If somehow he could invent a time machine, Newton could revisit the past.

It was a brilliant solution, with only one major drawback: scientists with much better credentials than Newton had been trying to invent such a device since forever and had failed spectacularly. From Archimedes to Copernicus to Dr. Fredrick Van Tulip, no one had even come close.

But did that stop Newton? No, it only made him concentrate even harder.

Fortunately he had a number of things working in his favour. Chief among these was a full laboratory, perched twenty stories off the ground, in a converted tree fort deep in the heart of the Merriwart kingdom.

As you may or may not know, the Merriwarts, a race of gentle giants, live in simple structures high among the colossal firs and cedars. Their kingdom can be accessed only by portal travel, and even then, it helps to have someone who's been there before show you the way.

In spite of the fact that to most people Newton looked like a regular kid (if somewhat small for his age), to the Merriwarts, he was a certified hero for saving their kingdom from the evil Liveds. Newton's act of bravery had earned their eternal gratitude, as well as his own Merriwart tree fort—a gift from Queen Gertrude. He was the first non-Merriwart ever to receive such an honour. Here Newton was able to set up his laboratory, free from the prying eyes and hands of his twelve-year-old quadruplet brothers—sports-crazed bullies who believed that tormenting ten-year-old Newton was fun and games.

As it was only a portal ride away from his bedroom to the

kingdom—he could be there in seconds—the lab had become
an ideal place to think, to dream and to tinker. After Newton
had moved all his inventing supplies, schematic diagrams and

journals to his tree fort, he rigged up four solar panels for power.

And that's where he had spent every free second for the past six months in pursuit of the impossible. He became so caught up in trying to construct the time machine that all the little distractions—clean clothes, tied shoes, mandatory bedtimes, vegetables—that can potentially drive a kid nuts, Newton hardly gave a thought to. Comic books, video games, writing in his journals and watching television were abandoned. Even when he wasn't physically in the tree fort, he was there mentally, going over circuit boards and wiring maps. All of his energy was channelled into attempting to create the greatest invention in the history of inventing.

"So what happens next?" Max asked. "Who's going to be the first to try this thing?"

Each of them looked at the others. "I guess I should," Newton declared. "After all, I invented it."

Gertrude stepped forward. "Nope. I will."

"You will?" Herbert asked, surprised.

"Of course. Can you send me back 310 years in time? I want to talk to my parents. Because they died on the day I was born, I never had the chance to know them. I have a few questions I'd like to ask."

"You're the Queen. Couldn't you get one of your subjects to do it?" Newton asked.

Gertrude stepped into the transporter. "Why let them have all the fun? No time like the present to visit the past."

Herbert squeezed in beside her. "I'm coming too," he declared. "I can't stand to be apart from you for one minute, let alone three centuries."

"Oh, Herbie, how romantic! Maybe you can still ask my father's permission to marry me."

"But we're already married. What happens if he says no?"

"How could he ever say no to a gorgeous hunka-hunka man like you? Don't be ridiculous."

"Are you two sure about this?" Newton asked, only because he wasn't too confident himself. "I was thinking maybe Max and I should try it out first. We're just kids. We're not that important."

"Speak for yourself," Max said.

"Don't be ridiculous," Gertrude replied. "It'll be a hoot. What could possibly go wrong?"

"Well . . . ," Newton began, but stopped. He didn't want to cause alarm by pointing out that given the complexity of the machine, in his estimation, roughly 1.2439 million things could go seriously awry. "I suppose it should be just fine. Though, you might want to plug your ears—the noise from the electrons could get loud."

"Don't worry, I haven't cleaned my ears in ages. I'll just move some of the wax around to block them up," Herbert assured Newton, and stuck his finger in his ear. Gertrude did the same.

Newton suppressed the urge to gag, turned the time-setting dial to 310 years, angled the pointer to BACKWARDS and input their destination. "Are you ready?" he asked. "Anyone need to go to the bathroom?"

"Sock it to us, Newton!" Gertrude replied, and hugged Herbert. "This is going to be fun-tastic! I always did feel a little . . . backwards."

"Okay, here goes. I'm activating the time-travel sequence." Newton set the travel sequence in motion. "Counting down, T minus ten . . . nine . . ." For the first couple of seconds everything seemed functional. Then Newton noticed wisps of black smoke wafting out of the control panel. The wisps quickly became clouds and soon the smoke engulfed everything.

Frantically Newton tried to stop the countdown. All the smoke made it almost impossible to see through the goggles, much less shut down the machine. Through the blur, Newton noticed dials spinning and pressure gauges creeping steadily into the red zone of HIGH ALERT.

Gertrude and Herbert had no idea anything was wrong, but Commander Joe saw Newton's face and was worried. "T minus six seconds. You should cancel the mission, Pokey."

"I'm trying to but I can't," Newton yelled. "Something's wrong!" A fact that was confirmed when the control panel burst into flames.

"GET DOWN, EVERYONE! HIT THE DECKS!" Commander Joe shouted.

The moment they ducked, the countdown reached zero and the machine exploded with a deafening *bang* that seemed to shake the very roots of the tree. The forest went completely silent, as if holding its breath. Nothing moved.

Soon, however, birds started chirping again and stunned

Merriwarts came out of their houses to see what had caused the commotion. Newton's ears were ringing. He was surprised that blood wasn't oozing from them. When the smoke cleared, he looked at the place where his invention had stood and discovered that it had completely disappeared.

Nothing remained but a gold, four-leaf clover and two burn marks in the wood. Everything was covered in soot.

Newton bent down and picked up the clover.

There was also absolutely no trace of the two giants. They had vanished, and Newton wasn't sure whether they actually had gone back in the past or been blown to smithereens.

Joe was in awe. "What happened? Do you think you . . . killed them?"

"I really need to go home, Newton. My mom told me to make sure I wasn't late for dinner," Max said nervously, obviously freaked out. Like Newton and Joe he was coated in soot.

Newton didn't say anything at all. He couldn't utter a word. His brain was on overdrive, trying to come up with a plausible explanation that didn't somehow result in Herbert and Gertrude dying. He had never felt worse in his life, though he was still in too much shock to cry.

He shuddered and put the clover leaf in his pocket.

CHAPTER 2

Lester, the Merriwart elder, was the first giant to swing over to Newton's tree fort. "Was that your time machine that I just heard?"

Newton nodded.

"So where is it?"

"I'm not sure," Newton replied sadly. "It sort of . . . temporarily disappeared. Apparently there are some bugs that need fixing."

"Don't be so glum, chum. If there's anyone who can figure it out, I bet my beard it's you," Lester said sympathetically.

"Thanks, Lester."

Lester grabbed hold of a branch and was about to boink back over to the main banquet hall, but he turned around and asked, "Oh, by the way, have you seen Herbert and Gertrude? Weren't they over here earlier?"

Newton gulped, and Commander Joe and Max looked

down, afraid to make eye contact with Lester. Should Newton tell Lester? What if Queen Gertrude's disappearance set in motion a major Merriwart panic? Still, he couldn't lie. "Actually they did stop by."

"Any idea where they went?"

"Honestly, I have no clue," Newton replied. And, technically speaking, that was the truth. He didn't. They could be anywhere. Assuming, of course, that they were *somewhere*.

"Well, if you see them, tell Gertrude to stop by the banquet hall. We've got plenty of work to do before the annual Festival of Hats." The Festival of Hats, set to begin in a week, was one of the highlights of the Merriwart year, and the party lasted four days. Queen Gertrude awarded a prize for the best hat and the everyone in the kingdom was preoccupied with trying to win.

After Lester left, Max turned to Newton. "Seriously, Newton. I need to get home."

"Quit your blubbering, soldier. We've got ourselves a situation," Commander Joe told Max. "Operatives have gone AWOL. It's our job to bring them in from the cold."

"They went somewhere cold?" Max asked.

"We don't know where they went," Newton replied dejectedly.

"But my mom is going to kill me if I miss dinner," Max insisted.

Newton looked at Max, trying to figure out why he was in such a hurry. Then he saw it. Max's . . . *problem* . . . with a nervous bladder had resulted in his needing a wardrobe change. "Okay, okay," Newton said. "But I've got to stick around and figure out this mess. I can't go just yet. If you promise to be really careful, I'll let you travel through the portal by yourself."

"Wow! You will? Of course I promise. Thanks, Newton."

Newton and Max went inside his tree fort, where Newton opened a trap door in the floor—the entrance to the portal that went directly into the tree in Newton's backyard. "Whatever you do, make sure you shut the door behind you once you get back." The last thing Newton needed was other humans discovering the portal and arriving in the Merriwart kingdom as tourists or loggers.

"Obviously. I'm no rookie," Max assured him.

"I know, but you can't be too careful." Newton didn't want to nag, but Max was pretty forgetful—even for a kid. Once he walked halfway to school before realizing that he had forgotten to change from his pyjamas into his school clothes. The entire school knew about the fashion faux pas before first bell.

Max climbed into the hole. "I'll give you a call later tonight. And don't worry, Newton, they'll turn up soon enough."

"No thanks to you," Commander Joe scoffed, as Max shut the trap door.

An instant later Max walked out of the portal door at the base of the oak tree at the far end of the Wigginses' backyard. The sight of the quadruplets totally threw Max off. They were trying to trap a skunk. Newton's older brothers had grand plans to release it into the girls' washroom at school the next day. Fortunately Max fled before they could torture him into revealing where he'd been.

But in his panic, he broke the cardinal rule of portal travel.

* * *

After Max left, Commander Joe was livid. "I can't believe the kid can just jump ship like that. I mean, we've got a situation on our hands and he's worried about cabbage rolls."

"Forget about it. We've got bigger problems than Max."

"But how can he be your best friend?"

"Listen, Max has issues. Deep down, he's nervous."

"I'm surprised he didn't wet his pants when your time machine exploded."

"He did. That's why he was so anxious to get home. I thought you noticed," Newton replied.

"Oh. Well, that's an entirely different matter. So maybe he has a nervous bladder. Poor kid. Stuff like that is tough on a soldier—especially in the field."

"His mother told him he'll eventually outgrow it. In the meantime, accidents happen."

"Speaking of accidents, you know, Pokey, it's only a matter of time before we have to tell Lester and the rest of the Merriwarts what happened."

Newton knew Joe was right. "Why did I let Herbert and Gertrude be the guinea pigs? Come to think of it, why didn't I just use a guinea pig? How could I have been so stupid as to test an invention on the Queen of the Merriwarts? My brain was obviously on vacation."

"Listen, don't blame yourself, Pokey. Even though it was your invention that caused this mess, moaning and blubbering will get us nowhere. A good soldier focuses on the future. 'Positivity' is our mantra. We've got to figure out how to get them back."

Easier said than done, as far as Newton was concerned. He didn't have a second time machine to go looking for them and couldn't very well waste six weeks building another.

His thoughts were interrupted by a commotion coming from the trap door. Suddenly four heads popped up from the hatch, each wrestling to be the first one out. Newton was so shocked to see his brothers, the quadruplets, in the one place where he honestly believed he was free from them that he gasped.

"So this is where you've been hiding from us," Engelbert smirked.

"We knew you weren't playing at the park," Earl said.

"We're going to tell Mom and Dad you're a liar," Eric added.

"And you'll probably be grounded for the rest of your life," Ernest finished off.

They started to climb out the hatch, but didn't get much farther before Newton yelled, "STOP RIGHT THERE!" Never in his life had he spoken to his brothers so boldly, but the thought of them trespassing in his tree fort quenched his usual timidity.

The quadruplets froze and looked at him in shock. "You can't possibly be talking to us. Can you?" Earl asked incredulously. The quadruplets were two times bigger than Newton, two times heavier and about ten times as tough. Plus there were four of them.

"I can and I will," Newton declared, trying desperately not to give away the fact that he was bluffing. "I've got bigger problems on my hands. Trust me, you have no idea what you're getting yourselves into. Option A: leave immediately. Option B: I take no responsibility for what may happen next."

"I'll take my chances," Engelbert said, and hopped out. His three brothers followed. They looked around in amazement at all the equipment. "What is this place, Newton?" Engelbert asked. "I mean, where are we?"

"A quadruplet-free zone," Commander Joe said. But because the quadruplets had virtually no imagination, they couldn't hear Joe, and therefore couldn't be offended. They actually thought he was a regular toy.

"Is this place yours, Newton?" Ernest asked.

"Yeah," Newton replied. "Listen, guys, I'm pretty busy right now and I would really, really appreciate it if you could maybe come back another time and visit."

"How does NEVER work for you? I think we can fit that into our schedules," Commander Joe offered.

"Sure, we could come back another time . . ." Engelbert began slowly, " . . . or we could stay for a while and have some fun. Come on, boys, get him!"

In a blur the quadruplets tackled Newton and had him tied up faster than a bull at a steer-roping contest. It was an awesome display of knotsmanship that left Newton completely immobile. Of all the lowdown unfair things to do . . .

"I declare this tree fort Quadrupletville!" Eric shouted. "From now on, no Newtons allowed!"

The quadruplets huddled, slapped their hands on top of one another's and shouted, "One for four, and four for one!" A tactical mistake that saw Lester boing back to Newton's tree fort, wondering what all the commotion was about. "What's going on in here?" the old giant demanded.

From his position on the floor, Newton was impressed with how intimidating Lester could sound. As this was the first giant they had ever seen, the quadruplets' cockiness was instantly replaced by knee-quivering fear.

"Let me guess," Lester said drolly, "these must be your brothers."

"Unfortunately, yes," Newton replied, wishing the old Merriwart didn't have to see him in this compromised position.

"Hey!" Eric said indignantly. "That's us you're talking about!"

Lester walked over to Eric. Though the quadruplets were big for their age, the giant towered over them. "Did you have anything to do with tying Newton up?"

Eric hesitated. Newton knew he was thinking about lying, but Lester's stare was boring holes in him.

"Actually, it was more of a group effort," said Eric.

Lester shook his head. "How utterly fascinating," he said sarcastically. The quadruplets smiled, apparently under the impression that he was complimenting them. "And if you don't mind telling me, where'd you get the brilliant idea?"

Eric looked pleased with himself and proudly admitted, "Well, when Newton is involved, who needs a reason—?" He barely got the sentence out before Lester snatched the boy up and held him upside down by the left ankle.

Eric's kicking and screaming hardly registered with the giant as he walked out onto the balcony. "Come along, boys, I want to show you something," Lester said casually, as if he were leading a birdwatching expedition. Ernest, Earl and Engelbert dutifully followed.

Commander Joe hopped with excitement in Newton's front shirt pocket. "Payback time, Pokey! I've been waiting for revenge since they imprisoned me behind the radiator for two years."

Lester continued. "I'm pretty sure you fellows aren't aware of this, but your brother, Newton Wiggins, saved the Merriwarts from certain extinction. As a result, we feel a little differently about him than it appears you do." Lester extended his arm and held Eric over the rail of the balcony.

Eric screamed, "Let me go! Let me go!"

Lester chuckled. "Oh, I'd love to. But as you can see, if I did that, well . . . you'd die."

The tree fort was nosebleed high. There would be brains all over the place. Eric started whimpering. The other quadruplets looked terrified.

Lester went on, "Now, listen closely, because I'm only going to say this once. I don't know what happened, maybe the four of you are so mean because you're sharing only one heart. But we've heard all about you and are far, far from impressed. I have half a mind to let go of your brother right now and watch him splat on the ground below, and then push the rest of you after him. I'm pretty sure the world would be a better place, and besides, I love oozing intestines. But instead, because I'm feeling rather generous, I'm going to let you off with a warning: the next time I find out you've been the least bit mean to Newton, it's over."

They gulped. "Over . . . ?" Engelbert quivered.

"Over," Lester replied. "I'll hunt you down, then eat you like a hamburger. And let's be absolutely clear, I will find out. Just try me." He dropped Eric onto the porch. "Now scram.

I've got important giant business to do. I don't ever want to see your ugly faces around here again. Oh, and the same thing applies if you breathe a word of this place to anyone."

The quadruplets practically knocked one another out in a mad scramble to get away from Lester and dive back into the portal. But before they could disappear too quickly, Lester stopped them.

"Excuse me! Aren't you forgetting something?"

The quadruplets looked at one another in confusion.

"I don't think so," Ernest said.

"Oh, I do. Apologize to your brother for tying him up," Lester said.

"Ask them to apologize to me as well!" Commander Joe shouted, for he knew Lester was sometimes hard of hearing.

"Sure thing. Apologize to Commander Joe as well!"

"Who?" Engelbert asked.

Lester picked up Joe and brought him to the boys. "He may be small, but he's the best Military Consultant we've ever had. Come to think of it, he's the only one."

Hearing the quadruplets apologize was something Newton had thought he'd never see in his lifetime.

He would have been able to savour it more if he knew where Herbert and Gertrude were. And if they were alive.

After Newton thanked Lester for untying him, the giant set off to find some phoenix feathers to decorate his hat for the festival. Newton examined burn marks on the floor where his time machine once stood, trying to figure out where he'd gone wrong—what had caused the spectacular meltdown.

"I don't understand this, Commander Joe. There were too many built-in safeguards for something like this to happen."

"And yet, it did," Joe replied ominously. "Are we talking sabotage here, Pokey?"

"Maybe," Newton replied, reluctant to blame an invention failure on outside forces. Still . . . nothing else made sense.

"You think a Merriwart did this?"

"No way. They couldn't. They don't have nearly enough technical expertise."

Newton was trying furiously to come up with an answer when he heard the blare of a trumpet—a sound he had never heard before in the Merriwart forest. He peered over the railing and far below he could make out a carriage, covered in animal skins, being pushed by four small creatures. Whatever they were pushing appeared to be extremely heavy, as they were straining to inch the vehicle forward.

"Looks like we have visitors," Commander Joe declared. "Let's investigate."

Newton and Joe weren't the only ones who scrambled down their tree trunk. It appeared as if the entire kingdom had heeded the trumpet call.

The carriage stopped, and the creatures, bent over and panting from their efforts, seemed glad for the rest. Barely taller than humans, their hands, ears and feet appeared completely oversized, almost clown-like. Given the scowls on their faces and their black smouldering eyes, though, they hardly seemed jovial. The tallest, a creature so dirty that

Newton wouldn't have been surprised to learn that untold colonies of small animals and bugs had taken up residence in his beard and hair, stepped forward.

"I am here to announce the return of Prince Raphael, twin brother of Gertrude!"

The Merriwarts gasped and immediately started buzzing with excitement. "Prince Raphael! Wasn't he eaten by a dragon?!" "Didn't he starve to death looking for the Leprechaun gold? Hadn't he promised we'd never have to see his droopy butt again?"

A groan emanated from the carriage. This was immediately followed by movement as the vehicle started to tilt precariously—Newton was certain it would topple. The groomsmen braced themselves against the side, their temples pulsating with the effort.

A hand emerged from the darkness of the carriage. The skin was mottled but stretched tight, as if super-inflated to the bursting point. It was fat beyond obese.

A leg emerged. Then the second. The groomsmen by now were trembling. Another groan came from the carriage, followed by silence. The upper part of his body was hidden behind an animal fur covering the door. What was Prince Raphael waiting for? A piglike snoring broke the silence. It seemed that the Prince had so exhausted himself in the effort to get out of the carriage that a nap was needed. The snoring grew louder. Merriwarts looked at one another in confusion. Should someone lend a hand?

Before a decision could be made, the carriage toppled over, landing on the groomsmen. Merriwarts rushed over and lifted the vehicle off of them. Though the creatures were dazed, they appeared unhurt.

Prince Raphael was now stretched out on the ground, and miraculously, he was still sound asleep, snoring so loudly that rainbow eagles were taking flight from the forest. One departing bird left a deposit that landed right on Raphael's forehead. Even the air bomb, special-delivered, didn't wake him.

Newton was shocked. The prince was, without a doubt, the fattest giant he'd ever seen. Instead of a neck, he had a quintuple chin. Fat hung below his tunic and settled against his knees. Newton wondered how the prince managed to avoid crushing himself with his own weight.

As suddenly as he had started snoring, Raphael stopped, opened his eyes (even his eyelids looked corpulent) and yawned. "Whew! It's been an exhausting trip! But it sure feels great to be home! I'm starved! What's for dinner? Where's Gertie?"

Lester stepped forward. "We thought you were dead. We haven't seen you since . . ."

"Blah. Blah. Blah. I know, forever and a century. And hello to you too, Lester. Speaking of dead, I'm surprised you're still kicking around. You were ancient when I left. Living on borrowed time, I suppose. Give me a hand up, boys!"

Raphael's four servants came over. They grunted and groaned and managed, with Herculean effort, to lift him to a standing position. He was almost as wide as he was tall, which for a giant, made Raphael positively enormous. He spied Newton and waddled over. "What are you?" he asked. "Dessert?"

"Newton Wiggins of 228 Bessborough Drive."

"Well, you look like Newton Wiggins of my dinner. Lester, let's say we cook this kid up. I'm going to disappear if I don't eat soon." With that, Raphael let out a huge burp.

Newton instantly felt woozy and had to step back for fear of passing out from the smell.

"My plastic's melting," Commander Joe declared, before sliding down into Newton's lab coat pocket.

"We will not be eating Newton," Lester said firmly, and then explained about Newton's heroics.

The story made Raphael roar with laughter, like it was the funniest thing he'd ever heard. Newton wondered if the effort of laughing might cause a heart attack.

Between gasps, Raphael managed to comment, "And to think that the fate of the kingdom rested on the shoulders of one kid. How pathetic! This place has gone downhill since I was around last. Next thing you know, Merriwarts will be living on the ground."

The other members of the kingdom clearly did not share Raphael's sense of humour and murmured their disapproval. For them, life out of the trees was a fate too horrible even to joke about.

Lester spoke up. "Well, obviously travel abroad hasn't smoothed out any of your rough edges. So to what do we owe this visit? Did you get lost? Because when you left, I believe you promised that we would never see you again."

"Let's just say I got a little homesick. I missed my bed. I do still have a bed, don't I?"

"As per your instructions, your tree fort remains untouched. Though, for a few years it smelled awful."

"Wow! I wouldn't have expected my slug stink-bombs to last that long," Raphael said proudly.

Lester ignored the comment. "I'm sure you heard that your sister finally married and is now Queen Gertrude?"

All at once Raphael's manner changed. His eyes narrowed, and in spite of all the fat, his face tensed up. "So then the rumours are true," he practically spat out.

"It was a glorious wedding. Your parents would have been proud," Lester declared.

Raphael was not impressed. "Did you know that there are some kingdoms where it's the firstborn son who becomes ruler and not simply the oldest child."

"Fortunately the Merriwart kingdom is not one of them," Lester replied stiffly.

Newton expected Prince Raphael to take offence to the remark, but instead the giant shrugged it off.

"Well, it gives me some comfort to know that when she's dead, I'll finally get to be King." And with that, Raphael fell asleep. He toppled onto his back and resumed snoring.

The alarm on Newton's watch started beeping. It was six o'clock. "Uh-oh, Lester, I've got to go. It's my mother's birthday. I absolutely can't be late."

"Don't worry, Newton," Lester assured him. "We'll be just fine here. I'm sure Raphael will stick around for a couple of days and then move on. The spoiled brat never liked us anyway. I just wish Gertrude would show up. She's the only one who can put the oaf in his place. Can you imagine if Raphael were our King?" Lester shuddered. "He'd destroy the kingdom within months."

"But why couldn't someone else be king? Like you?"

Lester laughed. "Don't be ridiculous. For thirty-three centuries Merriwarts have been ruled by the same royal bloodline. No exceptions. It's who we are. The throne has always had an orderly succession. And do you know what? Not once have we had a bad king or queen. We could never break that tradition just because Raphael might turn out to be an utter disaster." The giant shook his head as if ridding it of the horrible thought of King Raphael. "But there's nothing to worry about. Gertrude is our Queen and thank the leaves on the trees that she is nothing like her brother."

Newton swallowed hard. He'd have to do something—and quick. Usually his hyperactive brain would be debating the merits of different strategies. However, the shock of the day's events had clearly resulted in some sort of mind seizure, because the only thing he could think of was visiting his friend, Witch Hazel. For whatever reason, his deep subconscious was floating the idea that Hazel and her magical abilities might be part of a solution.

As Newton prepared to enter the trap-door portal, Commander Joe saluted him.

"I'm staying here, Pokey. While you're eating birthday cake, I'll do some reconnaissance work—see if I can collect evidence to verify your little sabotage theory on the time-travel disappearance."

"Good luck," Newton replied, before shutting the portal door.

Not that he didn't love his mom, but under the current circumstances, Newton wasn't in a party mood. Still, if he didn't show up, there was the slim chance that his parents might worry.

CHAPTER 3

Compared to the climbing walls, laser tag and renting out of go-kart tracks that were de rigueur for the quadruplets' parties, Mrs. Wiggins's fortieth was a tame affair. Mr. Wiggins had arranged for the town's top chef, Jean Marc, to come over and cook a meal. Considering his mom's awful culinary skills, Newton was actually looking forward to it. Unfortunately, Jean Marc specialized in sushi, and even an awesome display of slicing and dicing couldn't hide the fact that the result was raw fish. And Newton was no raw-fish eater. Much to the displeasure of the rest of his family, he had a peanut-butter sandwich instead—though Jean Marc insisted on personally cutting off the crust.

The quadruplets, still in shock after being chewed out by Lester, were surprisingly polite to Newton. So much so that Engelbert actually thanked Newton for passing him the wasabi sauce—without even being forced to do so.

Their father sensed something was amiss and asked Engelbert, "You all right, son? I don't know what it is, but you boys don't seem like yourselves today."

"I think they might be worried about the soccer tryouts," his mother offered. "After all, it's not every day that they get a chance to make history. All I can say is wow!"

"Nervous!" His father harrumphed. "With their skills, there is not a chance in the world they won't be going to Scotland this summer."

"But, dear," his mother continued, "they'd be the youngest players ever to make the national team. It's men against boys."

"It won't be a problem," Engelbert said confidently.

Newton didn't doubt him. The quadruplets were freaks for soccer and already had been the subject of countless television interviews and newspaper stories. An orange juice company promised them that if they made the squad, they would be in a commercial.

Newton's mother sighed with relief. "Well, that takes a worry off. I mean, I've already bought kilts for the whole family."

The quadruplets got up and started doing a jig around the table, singing, *"We're wearing kilts! We're wearing kilts!"* They couldn't have been more excited if their mother told them they were travelling to a distant galaxy on a research mission to find aliens.

Newton didn't share their enthusiasm. He felt he wasn't the kind of kid who could get away with wearing a kilt. There'd be laughter, definitely snickers. People might even conclude that he was weirder than they had suspected.

Jean Marc brought out the birthday cake (another disap-
pointment, as it didn't taste anything like a birthday cake),
and after Mrs. Wiggins blew out the candles, she announced,
"Thanks for the wonderful party! But I'm afraid it's time for
bed. We've got a big day ahead of us tomorrow!"

Newton was confused. Tomorrow? Tomorrow was Satur-
day. "We do?"

"Of course, dear. We need to be in Chestervale by nine-
thirty at the latest."

Chestervale was five hours away. "What for . . . ?" Newton
asked uncertainly.

The entire table laughed. "Haven't you been paying attention?" his father said. "Your famous brothers have their tryouts. It's been circled on the family calendar for months."

Newton turned and saw that, indeed, the date had been
circled. He had completely forgotten. An alarming oversight
considering he had a higher priority: to find Herbert and
Gertrude ASAP. "Do I have to go?"

His mother smiled at him sweetly. "No, of course you
don't have to go," she said. "You can stay here all by yourself for three days. I'm sure you'll have a great time."

Newton was flabbergasted. This was better than he had
expected. Maybe his family was finally starting to recognize
his unique needs. "I promise not to burn down the house,"
he assured them.

This produced a hearty round of guffaws from the table.
Newton couldn't understand what was so funny.

His father wiped a tear from his eye. "You're hilarious,
Newton. We know that you, of all people, wouldn't dream

of skipping the tryouts. How many times in your life will you get to witness greatness?"

"To bed!" his mother ordered jovially. "Alarm goes off at 4 a.m. sharp! Minivan pulls out at four-fifteen."

Newton lay in bed and waited, willing everyone to fall asleep. At ten-thirty he could still hear his parents packing downstairs. He wasn't the least bit tired. There was too much to do.

It was midnight before he was certain that everyone was down for the night, their alarm clocks set for four in the morning. Quickly he strapped on his homemade wings, opened his bedroom window and flew into the darkness. The wings were aerodynamic marvels. They worked even better than the first pair Newton had invented, and now he flew effortlessly through the night. The first time he had paid Witch Hazel a nocturnal visit, the flight had been terrifying. After all, Hazel lived on the edge of town, and the rumour was she ate children. As Newton discovered, the truth about Hazel couldn't have been more different. She was extremely kind, incredibly eccentric and knew more about the universe than a convention of Nobel Prize–winning scientists. In fact, Witch Hazel had been responsible for restoring Newton's imagination—a trick even Einstein would have done flips to learn. Over time she had become one of his closest friends.

Newton landed in Witch Hazel's front yard. The grass had grown longer and the house had become even more ramshackle since his visit last month. It appeared to be leaning to one side, ready to fall over. Witch Hazel prided herself on her ability to make a house look haunted, but the place was so derelict that Newton was worried she might have died. Cobwebs criss-crossed the front door and the python that usually guarded the doorbell was noticeably absent. Newton could feel a severe case of the heebie-jeebies coming on. Why hadn't he bothered to telephone Witch Hazel earlier to announce his visit—even for the sake of being polite?

"Witch Hazel? Oh, Witch Hazel!" Newton yelled after opening the front door and cautiously sticking his head inside. No one answered.

He turned on his headlamp and shone it into the living room.

A family of raccoons looked up at the light for a moment, then went back to picking at a carcass in the corner. They had the haughty demeanour of creatures who owned the place. Could it be that these were killer raccoons, a new breed so vicious that they ate humans, not garbage, and they were actually polishing off Witch Hazel's bones? Would they come after him next for dessert? Newton slowly backed out of the living room, never taking his eyes off the critters. He had to get back home. Since Witch Hazel was gone, he had no choice but to try to build another time machine. He had read that Einstein needed only three hours of sleep a night—he'd try to get by on one hour and work around the clock to build the machine.

"Newton Wiggins!" a voice cackled behind him.

Newton let out a scream, and the raccoons got on their hind legs and started viciously hissing at him. It took him a couple of deep breaths to calm down and discover that Witch Hazel was not only alive, but standing behind him. He was so happy to discover that she wasn't the racoons' midnight snack that he hugged her.

Hazel shooed him away. "Please, no hugging allowed. If this ever got out to the coven . . ."

"Sorry," Newton replied. "I thought the raccoons were eating your bones."

"Me? Ha! They're eating Mr. Feathers."

Newton gulped. "Mr. Feathers?" Perhaps Witch Hazel had taken a turn to the dark side and started killing off people in town.

She hadn't. Mr. Feathers was not a human, but a rooster that had been fattened up for Hazel's latest concoction—a cream to promote wart growth.

"Luckily my bats saw you flying here and told me, or we might have missed each other. I was out back gardening."

"Gardening?"

"Didn't you know that I'm a regular black-thumb? This year's crop of magic weeds promises to be the best ever. So, what brings you here?"

After Newton explained about the colossal mistake he had made with Herbert and Gertrude, Witch Hazel stroked the whiskers on her chin and hummed to herself, without so much as offering a sympathetic response. Newton waited. Minutes passed and still he waited.

When he couldn't stand it any longer, he finally asked, "Hello? Witch Hazel? Can you help me? Are my friends dead?"

His tone shook Hazel out of her reverie. "I have no idea. Time travel is way out of my league."

Newton slumped. If Witch Hazel couldn't help him, maybe he should just give up altogether.

"However, your situation isn't completely desperate. There is someone that we can talk to . . . in theory."

"What do you mean 'in theory'?"

"I had a little stalking problem with this character a while back. Let's just say he was a trifle overzealous in the love department. Couldn't take no for an answer. The last thing I'd want is for him to conclude that my heart's done a flip and we should start dating." Witch Hazel seemed to be weighing her decision. "On the other hand, you've landed in some serious crap-ola, so I have no choice but to help you. We can only hope I've become too ugly even for this Loverboy—he likes them gross!"

With that, Witch Hazel's broom appeared. "Let's go. Hold on to my waist, but be careful not to turn it into another hug."

Within moments they were airborne, leaving the lights of town behind. Newton looked at his watch. It was 12:55 a.m. He was way behind schedule. In a little over three hours his family would be leaving for the soccer tryouts. It was imperative that he return by 4:15 a.m.

"How long is this going to take?" Newton screamed over the wind, trying to make himself heard. They were now flying above a dark forest, the moon obscured by low clouds. He couldn't see a man-made light anywhere.

"We're almost there!" Hazel shouted back. "Just a couple more minutes and—" She pushed hard on the front of the broom and changed directions so abruptly that Newton was certain the centrifugal force had permanently displaced his brain.

"Sorry about that. I almost missed the turn," Witch Hazel screamed as they nose-dived, branches whipping against their faces.

Newton braced himself for the inevitable crash landing.

"HOLD ON, NEWTON!" Hazel shouted, as if Newton needed a reminder.

He was clinging to Witch Hazel as tightly as he could, like cooked spaghetti to a wall, desperately trying not to get flung off the broom. Hazel veered this way and that, taking a random pattern of turns that Newton had no way of anticipating.

Miraculously Hazel avoided crashing and skidded to a halt in a small clearing in a grove of cedars. They dismounted. Her hovering broom was twitching like an excited stallion. Hazel patted it affectionately. "Nothing like a night flight to soothe the spirit, don't you agree?"

Newton's head was spinning, like he had just gotten off the world's wickedest loop-the-loop roller coaster. He stared straight ahead in an attempt to make the dizziness go away. "I think I'm going to puke," he announced, and with that he hurled up his mother's birthday cake.

Witch Hazel was fascinated. "Wow! That's awesome! It's like you were possessed. What kind of spell is that?"

"The barfing spell."

"Can you teach it to me?"

Newton didn't have a chance to reply, because at that moment, out of the gloom of the forest hobbled a figure so hunched over, Newton couldn't tell who or what it was. It was wearing a black robe, the hood of which completely hid its head. Even when the creature looked up, Newton could see only a shadowy void where a face should be.

"Hazel, you old fright queen, to what do we owe this late-night visit? Perhaps a little smoochy-smooch?"

The deep voice calmed Newton immediately, and the dizziness that he had felt from the ride evaporated.

"Absolutely not! I'm here on business."

"That's what they all say, my lovely. Still, I've been aching for you something awful. Your warts have grown even more enchantingly disgusting."

Witch Hazel grabbed her broom and brandished it like a baseball bat. "Jules, I'm serious. Cut the romance or I'll send you to Jupiter."

Instead of being offended, Jules chuckled. "Nothing like the anger of a truly hideous woman to stir unmentionable thoughts."

"Jeepers creepers, Jules! I feel like I've been slimed. And not in a good way!" Witch Hazel shuddered before changing topics. "I'd like you to meet Newton Wiggins. Newton Wiggins, Jules La L'Arbre." Newton extended his hand to shake it, but the gesture caused both Jules and Witch Hazel to laugh.

"Jules isn't much for shaking hands. Come to think of it, Jules actually isn't much."

"Sadly, I've become a shadow of my former self," Jules joked, which caused Hazel and Jules to laugh even more.

Newton chuckled along with them to be polite, but had no idea what he was laughing about. He suspected that the joke might actually be on him, but he didn't mind at all now that Witch Hazel wasn't being freaked out by Jules's lovey-dovey advances.

Eventually they explained that Jules was a Trope, a creature who was virtually matter-less. No one could say exactly how old Tropes were (even Tropes themselves) but estimates had them making their first appearance at least six thousand years ago—and Jules was one of the originals. Tropes preferred to live alone and less than one hundred were scattered around the universe. As shadow-dwellers, they could blend in so perfectly with darkness that they almost always went unobserved. Sure, in cemeteries late at night or deep in the woods, Tropes tended to make their presence a little more obvious—tickling the necks of unsuspecting humans, breaking twigs or rustling leaves—but for the most part they preferred to remain undetected. Jules was wearing a robe only so that Newton could actually see where he was.

"Newton Wiggins," Jules said, all joking suddenly gone from his voice. "I'm not surprised to have you as a visitor."

"So you've heard," Witch Hazel confirmed.

"Yes, of course. First of all, congratulations on your time machine. You're a boy of exceptional abilities. No one in the history of the world, until you, has ever come so close to inventing such a machine."

"What do you mean 'come so close'? My machine worked."

Jules ignored the question. "You do realize the implications of a machine like that? How going back in time might profoundly affect the future?"

Newton didn't. He had just been hoping to see some dinosaurs.

Jules told him. "Here's an example: say you go back a couple of thousand years to look around. While there, you see a beautiful flower and pick it. What happens if that flower was the first of its kind and you prevented that species from existing?"

Newton would never do that; he was allergic to most flowers, and said so.

"That's not the point. Supposing the flower you picked was actually going to cure a future plague. Since it no longer existed, the plague wiped out entire populations." Like a kid who's just found out he's responsible for burning down his neighbourhood, Newton suddenly felt overwhelmed with dread.

"But that's not the worst part," Jules continued ominously.

Witch Hazel groaned. "Oh, for the love of fried slugs, do you need to be so negative, Jules?"

The Trope tsked. "I'll ignore that, dear. The worst part of your enterprise? You allowed the time machine to be stolen."

Newton shook his head. "No. It wasn't stolen. There was some sort of malfunction. The machine blew up and—"

"Not a trace of it was left. Trust me, what happened was no mere malfunction. There would have been debris all over the place, but instead, after the smoke cleared, nothing. It was stolen."

Newton instantly realized that Jules was right. Why hadn't

he figured this out for himself? "By who? There was no one around. I'm sure of it."

"You might be sure of it, but that doesn't mean you're correct. I hate to be the bearer of bad news, but Leprechauns stole your invention."

Newton remembered the four-leaf clover he had found after the time machine disappeared.

Witch Hazel groaned again. "Oh my! If those greedy creatures have your machine, we're done for!"

"My guess is that their plan is to go back in time and use their knowledge of the future to amass dizzying amounts of wealth," Jules said.

"And knowing Leprechauns, they won't stop until they have every last ounce of gold. Once the word gets out that they have this machine, the entire universal economy might collapse. Millions will be financially ruined."

"I thought everybody loved Leprechauns." Newton had grown up hearing tales of cute little green creatures chasing pots of gold and smoking pipes.

"That is so last century. Trust me, the way Leprechauns have been behaving lately, they're definitely not to be messed with," Witch Hazel informed Newton.

"What about Herbert and Gertrude. Do you know if they are still alive?" Newton asked Jules anxiously.

Jules sighed dramatically. "Who's to say? I haven't heard. In fact, that's the scariest part of all. You never know with Leprechauns. They're crafty. That's why they whisked Herbert and Gertrude away—to make sure you didn't suspect anything was amiss. But make no mistake: they're vicious enough to kill them."

"You wouldn't by any chance have something positive to say?" Hazel asked impatiently.

"I love it when you get annoyed. It makes the hairs on the end of your chin dance. Since you asked, there actually is a glimmer of hope."

"Come on, Jules, I know good news might kill you, but spit it out."

Newton leaned in closer.

"Your time machine doesn't work," Jules said, then added, "yet . . ."

Newton had never thought he'd feel so relieved that one of his inventions was a bust. Like all inventors, he prided himself on tilting at windmills, on tackling seemingly impossible problems. "Are you sure, Jules? I mean, I was ninety-nine point nine percent positive it was ready or I never would have tested it on Gertrude and Herbert."

"If there weren't glitches, we'd know it. There wouldn't be even a penny left to buy a crumb of bread."

The breeze picked up, colder and more ominous. An owl hooted and Newton had a sneaking suspicion that they were being watched. He looked around, and though he couldn't see much in the darkness, he could have sworn there was something behind a nearby tree.

"Did you see that, Jules?" Witch Hazel asked.

"Yes. Go now," Jules hissed. "Whatever you do, don't let them catch you, my love. We can always rendezvous later." With that he threw off his robe and vanished into the darkness.

The broom appeared and Witch Hazel got on it. "Quick, Newton, there's no time to waste!"

No sooner had Newton grabbed on to Hazel's waist than

they were airborne. Newton turned and saw that they were being pursued by at least a dozen Leprechauns, hunched over their broomsticks like kamikaze pilots.

"Newt's toes! When did Leprechauns learn to fly? They must have captured a loose-lipped witch."

Not only had Leprechauns learned to fly, but they had become ace aviators as well. They wore old-fashioned aviator goggles and helmets and hugged their brooms tightly to streamline themselves.

"The only question I have is, how did they find us? There's no way we were followed!" Hazel yelled as they streaked through the night sky.

No matter which way Hazel turned, the Leprechauns followed, matching her every move, never losing their perfect

V-formation. "I'm too young for this!" Hazel despaired. "I can't lose them."

Newton's teeth chattered from the speed and his cheeks felt like they were pressing against his ears. In a blink the Leprechauns had circled Witch Hazel's broom. They wore the traditional green suits, but even behind their goggles, Newton could see that their eyes burned ferociously. There wasn't a trace of merriment or Irish charm.

"Hand over the boy!" a Leprechaun ordered.

"I don't think so, short stack!" Witch Hazel replied, and then veered sharply upward.

As they rose the air temperature decreased dramatically. The lack of oxygen at this altitude soon had Newton gasping. If they went much higher, he was sure he'd suffocate— something he would have told Hazel if he had any breath left.

And still the Leprechauns gave chase. Newton knew it was only a matter of time before he died or the Leprechauns caught them. His lungs ached and his face and hands were numb from the cold. He wouldn't last much longer.

Holding on to the broom by one hand, Hazel fished into her pocket and took out a small packet. She held the package in front of herself and chanted, *"Rooster dead, the night is full of harm. Let the invisibility potion work its charm."* And then a cloud enveloped them.

Hazel pointed her broom downward and dove. They descended so quickly, Newton's stomach felt like it was going to burst out of his rear end. Fortunately, in an instant they reached an altitude where he could breathe properly again. Twice he had to swallow to pop his ears. When he looked up, he could see the Leprechauns were still after them. "I don't understand how they could still be on us. It's impossible. They can't see us."

Then Newton had a flash of inspiration. What if the four-leafed clover had something to do with their inability to lose the Leprechauns? The Leprechauns were able to track their movements so well—perhaps the clover had a homing device in it.

"Do you have another invisibility bomb?" Newton asked Hazel.

"Only one left. But we're already invisible, so I don't know what good it's going to do."

"As soon as they get close, drop the bomb and then turn sharply to the left. I've got an idea."

When the Leprechauns were once again breathing down their necks, Witch Hazel unleashed the invisibility bomb. At that instant Newton dropped the four-leaf clover.

When the smoke cleared, he saw the Leprechauns diving earthward. Newton and Witch Hazel were in the clear.

Back on the ground, in front of Witch Hazel's house, even after the invisibility bomb had been deactivated, Hazel was bent over, her hands on her knees, trying to catch her breath. "That was way too close for this old hag." She looked exhausted and haggard.

"What did they want?"

"Obviously the Leprechauns can't figure out how to fix the time machine by themselves. I'm willing to bet my last bottle of Troll spice that they were looking for a little handyman advice from you." Witch Hazel looked at Newton. "I don't want to think what would have happened if you were captured."

Newton shuddered. The ferocity of their eyes was tattooed on to his brain.

"We're all going to be deep in dragon dung—pardon the expression—as soon as they figure out how to work your machine. My guess is, if they can't find you, they'll kidnap some of the world's top scientists to help them out."

Newton shook his head. "All because I wanted to see dinosaurs."

As they stood there contemplating the fate of the world, Newton remembered the quadruplet's soccer tryouts. He looked at his watch. It was 4:14 a.m. One minute until his family's scheduled departure. Newton quickly strapped on his wings.

"Where are you going?"

"Listen, I've got to tell my family to leave without me."

The broom reappeared. "I'll give you a ride," Hazel offered.

Because he was in a hurry, Newton grabbed his wings and climbed onto the broom.

"Thanks, Hazel. But could you do me a favour? Don't let my family see you. They might lose their hair. Again."

"No imaginations, huh?" Hazel said knowingly.

"None whatsoever."

Witch Hazel dropped Newton off at 4:16 a.m. He was one minute late and he could see his family buckled into the minivan, ready to depart. They were waiting for him. Newton walked up to the driver's side window and tapped on it, nearly giving his father a heart attack.

"Where did you come from?" his father asked. Without waiting for a reply, he barked, "We're already behind schedule."

"I couldn't sleep," Newton lied, "so I went for a walk."

His mother sighed. "You know how I worry about you wandering around in the middle of the night. Get in the van, Newton, or we'll never make up the lost time."

Newton took a deep breath. "I'm not going."

The quadruplets, who Newton mistakenly thought were sleeping, opened their eyes and leaned forward.

"Did the punk just say what I thought he said?" Engelbert asked.

"Or was I having a nightmare?" Earl piped up.

"Maybe he had a lobotomy?" Eric suggested.

"Are we all absolutely positive he wasn't adopted?" Ernest added unnecessarily. They had been through the adoption issue many times before.

The side of his father's face twitched angrily. "Stop being ridiculous. You don't have a choice in the matter. IN! NOW!" his father ordered.

Newton couldn't recall ever seeing his dad so mad. It took all his courage not to follow orders.

"Listen," Newton began slowly and solemnly, "I'm only going to repeat this once: I'M. NOT. GOING!"

His family looked stunned, as if they had been zapped with 6,000 volts of electricity. It took them a couple of moments to recover from the shock, then his mother sputtered, "And why not, young man?"

"Because I need to save the world. That's why. Trust me, there's not going to be any world soccer championships if I don't get on it right now."

"He's insane," Ernest piped up from the back.

"And an idiot," Eric added.

Newton could see the whites of his dad's knuckles on the steering wheel. His father also appeared to be grinding his molars into paste as he worked himself into a rage. "WHAT'S WRONG WITH YOU! WE'RE ABOUT TO DRIVE INTO SPORTS HISTORY AND YOU'RE TALKING ABOUT SAVING THE WORLD?"

Newton decided to try a different line of reasoning. "You can sit here and argue with me for the next little while and miss the tryouts or you can deal with this when you get back. I'm ten years old and very mature for my age. What could possibly go wrong?" Of course, Newton could think of about ten thousand things. "Besides," he said, "if you force me to go, I promise that as soon as you stop, I'll just run away anyway and then you'll have to call the police and waste time looking for me instead of watching the quadruplets make the soccer team."

Newton knew his parents couldn't stand the pain that missing their glorious sports moment would cause. Just to be sure they wouldn't have any second or third thoughts, he added a small white lie: "And Max invited me to sleep over. I can stay at his place until you get back."

"You can?"

"Oh, definitely."

"You realize that when we return, you're going to be grounded?" his father warned.

"Possibly for life," said his mother.

Newton admitted that he did. His mother and father looked at each other and shrugged. He knew they could go either way.

"If Newton wasn't adopted, is there any chance at all that he was switched at birth?" Eric asked, interrupting their thoughts.

"No!" his parents both shouted.

Newton was actually relieved to hear their denial. He secretly feared this possibility. One day Newton would insist on blood tests to settle the matter once and for all.

His father put the van in gear. "We'll see you Tuesday. Don't use the stove or the washing machine!" he warned.

"And don't talk to strangers!" his mother cautioned. "

Newton assured them that he wouldn't.

"Good luck, fellows! I hope you make the team."

"Luck has nothing to do with it," Engelbert retorted.

"It's our destiny!" Eric shouted.

"Our birthright!" Ernest declared.

"We'll make the other players eat our shorts," Earl boasted.

With that, the minivan pulled out of the driveway and possibly into sports history.

Witch Hazel walked up beside him. "You have one weird family, Newton, and if a witch like me thinks so, it makes your family positively bizarre. Are your brothers always that nasty?"

"Sadly, even in their sleep," Newton replied.

"Someone should put a curse on them. Maybe give them pigs' noses or a third eye."

Newton brightened somewhat. "Maybe you could be that someone?"

"I could, but I won't. If the International Sisterhood of Witches found out—" She stopped and then continued on a different tack. "Well, let's just say witches have all kinds of ridiculous rules preventing us from cursing and hexing humans we don't much care for. Too restricting really, if you ask me."

Newton agreed. But in light of the fact that he had to save the world, putting a curse on his brothers seemed rather unimportant. "Hazel, I'm going to get the time machine back."

"How in the named of cursed cauldrons do you intend to do that?"

"The only way I know how. Face to face. Boy to Leprechaun."

Without waiting for Hazel's reply, Newton turned toward the house.

CHAPTER 4

"I might as well let them capture me," Newton explained to Witch Hazel, once they were inside. Since the Leprechauns were so intent on catching him, they must believe that he was the only person who could make the time machine work. Once in their clutches, Newton would trick them into thinking he was going to fix it, but instead, destroy his invention.

Hazel stroked her whiskers and pondered the logic of his plan. "You know, it has possibilities. But there are problems."

Newton couldn't think of any.

"What happens when they find out that you purposely sabotaged the machine?"

"I'll make it look like an accident," Newton assured her.

"What if they don't believe you? Once they have you, what's stopping them from torturing you until you build a machine that works?"

"I'd never do that!" Newton replied much more bravely

than he felt. Secretly he wondered what his breaking point was—he didn't have an exceptionally high tolerance for pain and suspected that his ability to withstand torture wasn't great. But then, maybe Commander Joe had some techniques that he could teach Newton.

"Nope. Your plan has too many risks."

Upon reconsideration, Newton reluctantly agreed.

The greys of dawn were just starting to creep into the living room. Hazel yawned, exposing a mouthful of rotting teeth. "Listen, Newton, I've got to get some ugly-rest."

"But what about the Leprechauns?"

"Don't worry. They can't get you."

"But we barely avoided their attack."

"They were only allowed to come after you because you were with me."

Newton didn't understand, and Witch Hazel had to explain that humans only became fair game when they portal-travelled with other creatures who could use magic. She was the link. "So absolutely promise me you won't portal-travel. You'll be snatched up in a second."

Not until after Newton pinky-promised (twice) and looked Hazel straight in her left eye was the witch convinced he wouldn't do anything stupid. She remounted her broom and zoomed off, leaving Newton to ponder his next move.

Though he was buzzing from the night's excitement, surprisingly Newton managed to get a couple of hours' sleep. It was still early when he awoke, but the shut-eye had given him another idea. He called Max.

His best friend sounded groggy on the other end of the line. Newton decided that he would not start Max's day off by rehashing the "accident" he had back in the tree fort.

"What's up?" Max asked.

Newton explained some of what had happened since the last time they were together. Then he said, "I need to ask you a favour."

"Does it involve danger?"

"Possibly."

"Then I'm your go-to guy," Max assured him. "I still feel bad about leaving the portal door open."

"Forget it. What I need you to do is go back to the Kingdom of the Merriwarts, and get Commander Joe and Lester and bring them here."

Max was now fully awake. "Sure. But why can't you do it yourself?"

"It's unsafe for me to portal-travel. I'll explain why later. Will you do it?"

"Sure. But don't you think it's dangerous bringing Lester into this world?"

"I'll take the risk." Newton's instincts were telling him that he needed to let Lester know what was going on. That keeping the giant in the dark about Herbert and Gertrude was no longer the right thing to do. As for Commander Joe, Newton felt he could use a military expert around, just to bounce ideas off. "I'm still figuring out the details. I'll update you later."

"What if Lester doesn't want to come?"

"He'll come."

From the moment Max left to retrieve Commander Joe and Lester, Newton paced back and forth in front of the oak tree in the backyard, wondering what was keeping them. After ten minutes he was convinced Max had gotten lost in the portal. At fifteen minutes, he was sure that Max had been captured by Leprechauns. At nineteen minutes, Newton told himself that if Max didn't show up in the next forty-five seconds, he was going after him.

Max popped out fifty-three seconds later.

"What took you so long?" Newton demanded, almost frantic. "And where are Lester and Joe?"

Joe, who had been hanging on the back of Max's shirt collar, walked onto his shoulder. "A little stressed out, are we, soldier?"

Lester tentatively poked his head out of the portal. He looked nervous. "Not many trees around here are there. Mostly shrubs." Of course to a giant from the Merriwart forest, even the hundred-year-old maple in Newton's front yard was a sapling.

"It's okay, Lester," Newton assured him. "You're safe. Quick, come inside the house before anyone sees you." The last thing Newton needed was his nosy next-door neighbour, Mr. Tagliano, finding out there was an XXXXL-sized visitor stomping around the neighbourhood. Mr. Tagliano would spread the word faster than a grass fire during a drought and before long the entire town would be in his front yard.

As they hustled Lester into the house, he banged his head

on the doorway so severely that blood gushed out and dripped on the carpet. And it got worse. The giant was not used to being in such a confined space and bashed a hole through the drywall with his elbow. This made Lester jumpier than a Chihuahua on a pogo stick and he tripped on the coffee table before taking out an entire shelf of china. Now fully panicked, Lester backed blindly toward the quadruplets' trophy shelf. Destroying fine china was one thing; wrecking the trophy shelf might result in Newton being kicked out of the Wiggins family.

Newton screamed "STOP!" as loudly as he could. "Don't move another step!"

Lester froze. He was shaking. "I'm so sorry," he moaned.

"Sit!" Newton ordered.

Lester squatted so suddenly that the floor shook and a five-foot-high karate trophy wobbled uncertainly before falling over. Luckily it didn't break.

"We've got bigger problems, Lester," Newton assured him. "My apologies for dragging you into this world, but I've been ordered not to use portal travel. It's a complicated story, but for now, there's something that I need to tell you." Newton paused. Lester looked at him expectantly. "I know what happened to Gertrude and Herbert."

Lester seemed amazed. "You do? Because frankly, I'm worried about Raphael. He's making noises, threatening that if Gertrude doesn't show up, he'll take over as Acting King until she does."

"Raphael can't do that! Gertrude's only been missing for a day!" protested Newton.

"You don't know Prince Raphael. From the moment he was born, he's been doing whatever he wants. This is so unlike Gertrude—I wish she had told us where she was going."

Newton tried to figure out a way to break the news to Lester softly. He couldn't. "I believe that they've been kidnapped by Leprechauns."

Newton instantly regretted the decision. Lester jumped up in shock and his head went right through the ceiling, then he crash-landed onto the coffee table. He suffered a large cut on his chin and he was dazed, but Newton was thankful that it wasn't worse.

"You might want to tell us the whole story while Lester is still a little out of it," Joe advised. "That way there's a better chance he won't destroy the rest of your house. Max, you should take a bathroom break. I've got a feeling this might get exciting."

"I'll be fine," Max said.

"I didn't mean any offence," Joe said sincerely. "Honest. I was just looking out for your interests."

Newton knew Joe was just trying to help. But a ten-year-old kid doesn't need help with that kind of stuff. He needs everyone to pretend that they never saw it. So Newton quickly launched into his story.

When he was finished, Lester couldn't stop blinking, as if his eyelids were helping his brain process the information. "Maybe it's the bump on my head, but this doesn't sit well with me. Are you sure Witch Hazel and Jules can be trusted?"

"She restored my imagination and Jules seemed to know everything already. So yeah, I'm pretty sure."

"Well, we've never had any problems with Leprechauns before. But then, we don't have any gold or diamonds. The only Merriwart who's ever been interested in that stuff is Prince Raphael."

As Newton mulled over the coincidence of Raphael's interest in gold and diamonds and the connection to the Leprechauns, they were interrupted by a knock on the door.

"Stay calm!" Commander Joe ordered. "We could have a situation on our hands here. Pokey, you take the door. I'll cover your back. Max, you watch Lester."

Two police officers stood at the door. They looked big and like they were itching to arrest someone. Their name tags read OFFICER HUGO and OFFICER FRANCES.

"Hey, kid, are your parents home?" Officer Hugo asked Newton.

"No. Is there a problem?" Newton asked innocently.

Officer Frances flipped through her notebook. "Noise complaints. Neighbour was 'terrified'—direct quote—that something awful was happening. What's your name?"

"Newton Wiggins. There must be a mistake. I'm doing homework. I don't even have the television on. My parents are away for the day at soccer tryouts," Newton replied.

"Soccer tryouts? Don't tell me you're related to those quadruplet brothers?" Hugo asked, a hint of excitement creeping into his voice.

Newton affirmed that indeed he was.

"Wow! Congratulations. You must be so proud," Officer Frances said. "Those kids are going to put us on the map!"

"And get their own orange juice commercial!" added Officer Hugo.

To distract the officers, Newton could have shown them the trophy room, but with Lester sprawled out on the floor, he didn't think it a wise move.

Officer Hugo looked at him suspiciously. "So why aren't you at the tryouts cheering your brothers on? You realize that half the town left for Chestervale?"

"Yeah. I know . . . you see . . ." Newton stalled. " . . . I have to finish this huge homework assignment," he lied. As soon as the words were out, he realized that it would have been better not to say anything at all.

The officers looked liked they had just eaten leech stew. "Homework to finish? Of all the lame excuses . . ."

"I should arrest you for bad sportsmanship, but unfortunately there's no law against it," Officer Frances spat out. She shook her head like a dog coming out of the water, trying to rid herself of the terrible thought of Newton's lame homework excuse. "Mind if we take a look around? Make sure everything's okay here?"

"Uh, I don't think that would be such a great idea," Newton said, trying to block their path.

"And why not, Homework Boy?" Officer Hugo asked, all trace of friendliness gone from his voice.

Newton didn't even have time to cook up another lie, because a tremendous crash came from the rear of the house. Officer Hugo and Officer Frances looked at each other and when they turned back to Newton, he was already racing toward the sound of the destruction, praying that Lester hadn't taken out the trophy room.

He hadn't. Instead the giant was sprawled on the outside deck, blood trickling from his hands and face, the result of inadvertently walking through the patio doors. "Are you all right, Lester?" Newton, asked, bending over the fallen giant.

"I'm fine," Lester groaned. "What happened?"

Before Newton had a chance to reply, Officer Frances, gun unholstered, shouted "NO ONE MAKES A MOVE!"

Officer Hugo was also nervously waving his firearm around. "YOU HEARD THE LADY! I DON'T WANT TO SEE EVEN SO MUCH AS A FACIAL TIC!"

Max, who had left the room to find some bandages, made the mistake of stepping on a piece of glass and loudly crunching it on his return to the room. The noise startled everyone and Officer Hugo mistakenly fired his gun. The bullet just missed Lester's ear.

Frances looked at Hugo sternly. "Be careful there, Officer."

Hugo sheepishly apologized. "Don't tell the chief about this. Please. I honestly didn't mean to shoot."

Commander Joe, who was still on Newton's collar, spat in disgust. "Mistakes have no place on the battlefield—someone could have been killed." Of course the officers couldn't hear him.

"Don't sneak up on us like that again, kid," Officer Frances told Max. "You have no—" She stopped abruptly when she saw the stain.

Max had done it again. Under the circumstances, who could blame him?

Everyone looked away. "I've got to go home," Max said, then dropped the bandages and took off.

Newton didn't have time to worry about Max, because Officers Hugo and Frances quickly moved in to handcuff Lester. (Their regular handcuffs were too small so they had to use plastic cables.) Newton demanded to know what Lester was being charged with.

"Listen, Newton, this creature trashed your parents' house, and has three toes and no identification. He's coming downtown," Officer Frances replied. "A judge will decide how long he should stay in jail."

By the time Officer Hugo and Officer Frances (along with eight more backup police officers who were called to help) stuffed Lester into the paddy wagon, he was beside himself. His eyes looked wild. "What's happening, Newton?" he asked, frantically straining against the bars of the wagon's window.

Newton thought he might be sick, seeing Lester like this.

"Easy, easy there, Lester," Newton replied, trying to soothe the giant. "They're taking you to jail. But hopefully not for long. I'll get you out."

Because Merriwarts didn't have prisons—instead they had various other punishments including being banished from the kingdom—Lester didn't know what jail was, and Newton had a difficult time making him understand the concept.

"But I need to be back in the trees. Among my people. Please tell them that, Newton!" Lester wailed when he finally started to comprehend where he was going.

After the police had gone, Newton and Commander Joe surveyed the destruction in the Wiggins house. There was no way it could be put back together.

"Lester really did a number on this place," Commander Joe remarked. "But look on the bright side, imagine how much worse you would feel if the trophies had been totalled."

Newton was exhausted, not just because he hadn't slept much, but because so much had gone colossally bad in less than twenty-four hours. If he had tried, Newton doubted he could have done a better job of botching things up. What was wrong with him? Never had he felt so awful. A tear rolled down his cheek, quickly followed by another and then another and pretty soon the blubbering was full-on.

Commander Joe climbed up on his shoulder. "That's okay, Pokey, today's soldier is encouraged to show his emotions," he said gently.

"I only have myself to blame for wrecking everybody's life," Newton cried ruefully, by now feeling sorry for himself.

"That's one way of looking at it," Joe replied. "The other way is to say that we've made some tactical errors but fortunately we've got more moves than a chess master. Don't tell me we're done yet. Because if that's the case—" Joe paused, went over to the stereo and put on a rousing piece of music, Tchaikovsky's 1812 Overture, and turned the volume up LOUD.

Shouting over the music, Commander Joe continued. "If that's the case, then I'm searching for a new Newton. Because the boy I know would look mistakes in the eye and

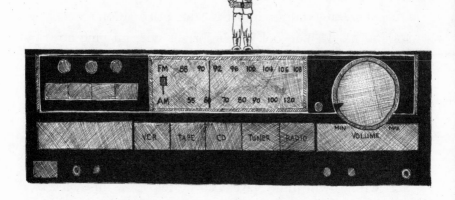

roar, never letting a few speed bumps on the road to saving the world slow him down!"

No one could give an inspirational speech like Commander Joe. It was impossible for Newton to keep feeling sorry for himself in light of such stirring oration. He wiped away his tears, sniffled and said, "Okay. I'm better. The pity party's over. What's our plan?"

Commander Joe turned off the music. "I don't have the faintest idea."

Hours later, after most of the mess had been cleaned up, there was another knock on the door. Newton opened it to discover that Max was back, this time wearing a fresh pair of pants.

"I'm in," he declared.

"In for what?" Commander Joe asked.

"Whatever's coming our way, I've decided to stick this one out to the end. And . . ." Max hesitated. "I brought extra underwear."

"Congratulations. A soldier can never be too prepared," Commander Joe said.

Newton was thrilled to have his friend back. "We could use an extra man on this mission. Welcome aboard."

Max pulled a thick book from his army knapsack. "I thought that this might come in handy. It was my grandmother's." Max's grandmother, Dr. Lucy Franklin, had been a world-famous anthropologist—she once even had tea with the Queen—with a remarkable knack for unearthing lost treasures. Sadly, her career was cut short when her research ship sank in the treacherous waters rounding Cape Horn. Her legacy resides in museums around the world, and a shelf of books that were given to Max's mother.

The tome looked about two thousand years old. Newton wouldn't have been surprised to see the pages stuck together with cobwebs. He wiped the dust off the cover and read the title. *A History of Ireland: The Unauthorized Version*. It was written by the Brothers Grimm, the same guys who penned "Little Red Riding Hood" and a bunch of other famous fairy tales.

"I don't think we have time for bedtime stories," Newton declared.

"Open it up to chapter seventeen," Max replied, ignoring Newton's comment.

Setting the book down on the floor, Newton started

thumbing through it. Dust rose up from the pages and caused him to sneeze.

"Sorry about the dirt. I've tried to clean the book off a couple of times, but it's weird how quickly it goes back to grimy."

Chapter seventeen was called "Leprechauns in Their Natural Habitat" and Newton flipped through the pages quickly. A lot of words were spelled the old-fashioned way, but aside from that it was quite easy to understand what was written. He stopped speed-reading when he came to the section detailing the exact location of these legendary creatures.

To find Leprechauns one must journey to Macgillycuddy's Reeks
Travel deep into the mountains, o'er the peaks.
Drop into a valley that hase no name
That doesn't exist but is there all the same.
You'll need to be bright and wyse and very brave
To find the gold that these creatures crave.

Newton looked up from the book. "Can this be trusted?"

"The Brothers Grimm were first and foremost scientists. My mom says Grandma Lucy made many of her discoveries using this book as a guide."

"I assume the mountains of MacGillycuddy's Reeks are in Ireland?" Newton asked, pondering the implications.

Max nodded. "Right in the middle of the country. I found it in the atlas before I came over."

"Well, the Leprechauns would never expect us to go looking for them, would they?" Newton wondered.

"Not likely," Joe agreed.

"If the element of surprise is on our side, we just might have a chance to rescue Herbert and Gertrude," Newton concluded, all but ignoring Witch Hazel's earlier warnings about the Leprechauns. "It's off to Ireland!"

Commander Joe jumped up and down excitedly. "We're taking it to the enemy! I like your style, Newton. I like your style." He stopped jumping. "But what about Lester? We can't leave him in jail."

Joe was right. At this moment, Lester was probably thrashing around in a cell, wild at being confined, not fully understanding what had happened to him. And if Officer Frances and Officer Hugo were any indication, he wasn't likely to be released anytime soon.

"We'll get Hazel to help us break him out."

Commander Joe, Newton and Max stared at Witch Hazel's house in disbelief. Flames licked out of every window. A crowd had gathered to watch as two fire trucks fought a losing battle to contain the blaze. Newton knew it would be only a few minutes before the whole house went up in a huge whoosh. He tried to convince himself that there was no way Witch Hazel was in there, but he couldn't be sure. After all she had gone home to get some ugly-rest.

Newton walked over to the fire chief. "Did you notice if anyone left the house?"

"I have no idea, kid," the chief said gruffly, "and this fire's still way too hot to take a look inside. We won't know for hours."

"Has Witch Hazel been seen?"

"Who?" the chief asked, obviously irritated by Newton.

"Witch Hazel. The person who owns the house."

Another fireman, his face grimy from the smoke, walked up to them. "Witches? Hazel Scuttle lives here. Trust me, she's no witch. Besides, the neighbours who called in the fire say they haven't seen anyone."

As Newton turned and watched the roof collapse, Commander Joe said, "I'm sure she made it out alive."

Newton wasn't so certain but dared not consider the possibility. He couldn't afford tears. Not now.

What had started the blaze? Faulty wiring? A potion gone wrong?

Or was it the Leprechauns?

CHAPTER 5

"Since Witch Hazel told us not to use portals, we'll have to travel the regular way," Newton informed Max and Commander Joe. They had returned to his house to strategize. They agreed that Lester would stay in jail while they concentrated their efforts on Gertrude and Herbert, because they could only solve one giant-problem at a time.

"Ireland is over four thousand miles away. What's the 'regular' way?" Max asked, sounding slightly worried.

A good question. One that Newton had been thinking about for the past hour. He explained that the obvious choice was to buy a plane ticket. But since Newton didn't have a passport—a necessary requirement for international travel—that option was ruled out. Even if he did, tickets would be way too expensive.

"What are the chances of us stealing a plane?" Commander Joe asked. "Under the War Code such actions are legal."

Max shook his head. "They guard those things pretty closely. There's no way we'd get away with it."

Then Newton had an idea, one so absolutely preposterous that he thought it might work. "What's stopping us from FedEx-ing ourselves over to Ireland?"

"You can't be serious," Max asked.

"I admit, the plan is slightly dangerous and there's every possibility that we will get caught—but why not? We pack ourselves into reinforced boxes, write FRAGILE on the outside, call FedEx, and we're there by ten o'clock the next morning. Guaranteed. What do we have to lose?"

"You know, Pokey, I like your moxie," Commander Joe said. "Reminds me of the Banana War in '63. We slipped unnoticed into North Africa packed in orange crates. They never saw us coming."

Max took some convincing, but when Newton challenged him—come up with a better plan—he eventually agreed that this was their only chance of reaching Ireland in time. Still, the whole thing almost came unravelled in the execution. It took all of Newton's inventiveness to devise a proper method of packing them safely into the box. They had to work quickly as the FedEx pickup was scheduled for four-thirty—less than forty-five minutes away.

While Newton was reinforcing the cardboard, Max searched the Internet to find a suitable shipping address. He decided on Killarney National Park, located on the edge of Macgilly-cuddy's Reeks. It seemed as good a place as any, exotic even.

Max stared at the shipping forms. "It says I also need a contact name."

"Put 'Park Ranger.'"

"What if they don't have a park ranger?"

"They'll have one," Newton assured him.

"What about contents? What should I write in that space?"

Newton didn't want to arouse suspicion at Customs by listing "Two boys and a live action figure" as the goods being shipped.

"Write 'Oranges,'" Commander Joe replied. "It worked for me once. Why shouldn't it work again?"

After packing peanut butter, clothes and taking bathroom breaks, they only had minutes to spare before the pickup. As Commander Joe performed the last bit of duct-taping, Newton and Max lowered themselves into the box. They wore helmets, and knee and elbow pads to protect against the inevitable bumps. Just as Joe was squeezing himself in an air hole Newton had made in the box, the FedEx van pulled up.

"No one says a word," whispered Newton. He could hear the FedEx man grunt and curse about the weight of the box. Newton thought his tailbone might crack as the box bump-bump-bumped down this front steps. Max groaned. Newton dared not ask if he was all right.

Maybe it was the size of their cargo, or perhaps the delivery guy was illiterate, but he clearly ignored the FRAGILE stickers that Newton had conspicuously slapped all over the outside of the package.

Only after he heard the back doors of the truck shut did Newton feel it was safe to start talking. "You all right, Max?" he whispered.

"I think I broke my bum," Max replied.

"Keep it down, soldiers," Commander Joe ordered, "we're on Code Purple."

Newton didn't know what Code Purple was, but decided to follow Joe's instructions.

As the hours rolled by, Newton started to wonder if the driver had a route that covered half the country. Both he and Max were cramped. Every muscle was long past the point of hurting and severe numbness had set in. Max was doing his best not to complain, but occasionally he couldn't help it.

"I won't be able to last all the way to Ireland," he informed Newton.

"Don't worry. As soon as we're loaded onto the plane, you can get out and stretch," Newton promised.

In the darkness of the plane's cargo hold, Commander Joe finally gave the okay to climb out. He had expertly sliced through the duct tape with his hunting knife. They had been confined to the box for more than four hours. It was a good twenty minutes before either Max or Newton could properly move again. Both put on their headlamps and looked around. Boxes were piled everywhere.

"Those cargo handlers should be fired," Max said, tentatively rotating his arms, "I'm surprised my ribs aren't broken."

In spite of the soreness, Newton was thrilled. He had never travelled cargo before. "I can't believe we made it! I thought for sure they'd open the box."

"Good strategy, Pokey! A four-star general wouldn't have come up with a better plan."

"I have to admit, you did it, Newton," Max agreed. He pulled out his cell phone and started to dial.

Newton asked who he was calling.

"My mother. She's probably already worried and is going to want to know where I am."

"Again, I must remind everybody that we're Code Purple. Which means no civilian contact until the mission is over," Commander Joe stated.

"Sorry. I have to call. I promised."

"But what are you going to tell her?" Newton demanded.

"The truth, that we're trying to save the world using Grandma's book."

Newton's flashlight beam caught the look of determination on Max's face. It would be pointless to argue. Max was not going to back down.

"Okay, go ahead. Make it quick," Newton said resignedly.

"Whatever you do, don't tell her our coordinates," Joe warned.

His mother wasn't home, so Max left a message explaining that he'd be out of the country for a while and that she shouldn't worry. If he got the chance, he'd try to call her again, but there was every possibility he'd be unable to. His cell phone probably wouldn't work overseas.

After eating peanut-butter sandwiches and drinking juice

from drink boxes, Newton and Max lay down. In spite of the cold and noise of the cargo hold, they managed to sleep. Because Joe was made of plastic, he didn't need to rest (though occasionally he did, when he was in the mood). He said that he would give them fair warning when they were about to land, so that they could repack themselves.

As luck would have it, a Killarney park ranger actually existed. Mr. Jerry O'Brien signed for the unexpected package. Unfortunately, Jerry was an ancient man who suffered from a rather fickle heart. When he opened the FedEx box and poked his head inside, the shock of seeing two boys smiling up at him sent the poor man's ticker into overdrive and he promptly keeled over.

By all appearances it seemed that Newton and Max had killed Killarney's oldest citizen and only park ranger.

Death tickled Max's bladder reflex and he had yet another accident (understandable given the circumstances). Meanwhile, Newton bent over and listened for the old man's breathing, but couldn't hear anything.

"I'm pretty sure he's dead. What do you think we should do?" Newton whispered.

"Get out of here pronto. This guy was already three feet under. His time was obviously up. We had nothing to do with it—simply victims of being in the wrong place at the wrong time," Joe declared. "So I say let's move it out, soldiers!"

Newton was about to protest, when he thought he saw a twitch in the man's left cheek. Though it might have been his imagination, Newton didn't want to take a chance. He started administering mouth- to- mouth—completely grossed out that he might just be kissing a dead guy—and kept at it until the man started coughing. Newton backed off when Jerry O'Brien sputtered violently, sounding like he was trying to hack up a phlegm ball.

When the park ranger finally regained his senses, he shook his head in amazement and asked, "What happened? There was a white light and the most peaceful music I ever heard. Then I dreamed that my dear, dead wife was kissing me."

"You just about died," Newton said. "But I saved your life."

Jerry O'Brien spat on the floor in disgust. "Saved my life! Bah! I'm 101 years old and way past ready for death. I've been waiting sixteen years to join my Maggie upstairs. To think that it could have been all over and you ruined it! Argh! Here's a word of advice: next time someone's halfway to dying, leave them alone!" The old man rose slowly and uncertainly to his feet. Newton would have helped, but Mr. O'Brien gave the distinct vibe that he was not a person who would appreciate assistance. "I'm going to the pub!" Jerry harrumphed. He grabbed his cane and walked bowleggedly out of the office.

"Well, at least that crackpot's out of the way," Joe declared. No sooner had he said this than a huge woman who could barely fit through the doorway entered the office via an entrance from the far end. She was accompanied by three angry-looking sheep.

"WHO ARE YOU!" she bellowed.

Joe quickly ran into Newton's shirt. The woman wore filthy overalls and a tank top. Her hair was red and she looked like she had a temper to match it.

73

Neither Newton nor Max spoke. One of the sheep *baaed*.

The woman came closer and Newton could smell that she'd been around animals—a lot. Manure was caked on her boots and hands.

"I SAID, WHO ARE YOU!" she yelled, this time much fiercer.

Newton was pretty sure that if Max hadn't just had an accident, this would make his nervous bladder sing.

"I'm Newton Wiggins, and this here is my friend, Max Brown. Who are you?"

"IRRELEVANT! WHERE'S MY GRANDFATHER?" the woman yelled, completely ignoring Newton. "My sheep are waiting. I've no time to waste. I need to get out of town before I get a rash." She started scratching the back of her neck so energetically that Newton wouldn't have been sur-prised to see blood.

"The old guy? He went to the pub."

"The pub? Oh sweet mother of Mary! That'll be the death of him! Grampy's got a bad ticker, don't you know?"

Newton was about to tell her that he actually did know this about her grandfather, but the woman turned and left—most likely in the hopes of saving Jerry O'Brien's life once again.

"Let's get out of here," Joe urged. "Before another lunatic from the official welcoming party discovers us."

Killarney was a quaint town that obviously catered to tourists. It seemed like every second store on the main street was a gift shop selling postcards and fudge. The visitors agreed to walk purposefully, as if they knew exactly where they were going. Of course they had no idea, except that they could see the mountains at the far end of town. As they moved along, Newton reread the directions from *A History of Ireland: The Unauthorized Version* that he had copied from Dr. Lucy Franklin's book. The prophecy was maddeningly vague.

To find Leprechauns one must journey to Macgillycuddy's Reeks
Travel deep into the mountains, o'er the peaks.

When they had gone a few hundred yards past the last cottage and were staring at the foothills to Macgillycuddy's Reeks, Commander Joe pulled out a map and a compass. "By my calculations, from here, if we walk northeast, we should reach the heart of the mountains before nightfall."

"What calculations are you using?" Max asked testily. "Because I'm telling you right now, I really don't want to die of starvation on the side of some desolate mountain in Ireland because you mistakenly read the map upside-down."

Commander Joe took his mapmanship very seriously. "If my expertise as a Secret Agent Superstar trained fighting machine who just happened to win first place in the SAS Orienteering Challenge three years in a row isn't up to your standards, why don't you lead us on, Magellan," Joe huffed, and held out the map for Max.

Before Max could grab the map and completely offend Joe, Newton interjected. "There's no need for that. Commander Joe's the best in the business. End of discussion.

Let's focus. We lose sight of our goal and it might be a global catastrophe."

Thankfully Max kept his mouth shut. But Newton mentally noted his friend's increased irritability. Add to this, Max's face was considerably paler than when they had left home. Dark circles had formed under his eyes and he sounded like he was in the initial stages of laryngitis. All classic signs of homesickness.

Newton suddenly remembered that Max had been affected by the disease severely in the past. Even on campouts in the backyard, only ten yards away from his kitchen, Max complained about insomnia and usually abandoned the tent for his bedroom before midnight. Max's week at overnight camp had lasted only until sunset the first day before his parents were called and he was taken home. Somehow, Newton had forgotten all about Max's separation issues before inviting him along on the adventure.

As Joe continued to study the map, Newton took his friend aside. "How you feeling?" he asked gently.

"Not good. I was thinking that maybe I should call my mother. Just to see how she's doing," Max whimpered.

Full-blown blubbering didn't appear to be too far off. Newton instructed Max to take out his cell phone. "Look, there's no service. You couldn't call even if you wanted to."

"What about a pay phone? Maybe I could call her from there." Traces of hysteria were now edging into Max's voice.

Newton grabbed his friend by the shoulders and looked him in the eye. "Listen to me: we're too far away for your mother to come and bring you home, so stop thinking about it. The earliest she could possibly get here would be tomorrow. By that time, this will be all over."

"Promise?"

"I promise," Newton lied. The problem with saving the world was the extreme difficulty of pinning down how long it might take. But Newton couldn't see the advantage of letting Max in on this fact.

At the edge of town, past the last cottage, only one trail led into the mountains, so they took it. Though they were weighted down with knapsacks, the footing on the trail was easy and they were quickly over the first couple of passes. Newton was almost enjoying himself because the walking was easy along the grass-lined hills. There was something to be said for seeing new places. If he ever made it out alive, Newton would highly recommend to his family that they take a trip here.

After lunch he began feeling differently. The weather had turned colder and rain was falling. At first it was just a drizzle, but soon it came down hard. The trail had narrowed and was rising steeply. Twice Newton fell, and now he had a deep cut on his left shin. Max ripped his pants after landing on a sharp rock and it was all he could do to not cry.

"Pokey, we've got to find shelter," Commander Joe said. "Me, I'm fine, of course. My plastic can take anything except extreme heat. But I'm worried about you two."

Newton looked farther up the trail. It seemed to disappear in the fog. He had been so intent on watching his footing that he failed to notice the decreasing visibility.

"Are you suggesting we just stop here and lie down for the night?" Max asked anxiously, shivering. "We'll die." Max's rain jacket obviously had limited waterproofing abilities.

"Relax, Max, it'll be okay."

"No, it won't!" Max shouted. "No, it won't! We're going to get eaten by bears and die!"

Commander Joe laughed (a little too heartily, Newton thought). "Everybody knows there aren't any bears in Ireland. Snakes either, for that matter."

This wildlife factoid had no effect on Max's disposition. "I don't care. Something bad is going to happen, I can feel it in my ears. Why I ever let you guys convince me to come here, I'll never understand."

"What are you talking about? You begged us to come, don't turn the tables now, soldier," Commander Joe said testily.

Once again Newton stepped into the fray. "Forget about it. Max, get a grip. Commander Joe, stop arguing with him. It's not helping." Newton hadn't bargained on having to assume parenting duties on this trip.

Commander Joe tucked himself back into Newton's shirt, and Max sulkily turned to face the town—or rather, to face where it was supposed to be. They couldn't see the town or much else because the fog was growing thicker by the moment. Newton doubted it would lift before nightfall, but they couldn't just wait it out—not with Max on the verge of a full-blown freak-out. Yet to continue climbing blindly seemed equally foolhardy. As Newton tried to figure out the best of the worst alternatives, he heard a sound that made him shudder: voices of children were crying.

They drifted hauntingly through the fog, faint, but unmistakable.

"Does anybody else hear that?" Newton asked nervously. Was there a mountain ogre close by torturing kids, preparing them for a stew?

"We're going to die," Max stated.

Another voice drifted through the mist, this one slightly louder and slightly sadder than the last. Newton figured a kid was most likely tied up and being forced to watch his sister get boiled alive—maybe even skewered to be roasted.

"Sounds like sheep to me," Joe declared.

"You sure it's not a kid?" Newton asked.

"Yeah, it could very well be a lamb. I'd have to be closer to know for sure."

Another cry was heard and now Newton knew that Joe, thankfully, was right. It was definitely sheep, not children, that he heard bleating through the fog.

In his relief, Newton had an inspiration. "If there are sheep, what is usually close by?" he asked excitedly.

"Wolves, coyotes, rabid dogs," Max answered.

Newton hadn't considered those unwelcome neighbours. "Yes, well, potentially. But I was also thinking there might be a shepherd or two looking after them."

"I like your logic, Pokey," Commander Joe said. "Someone who knows the lay of the land."

"Or can't see us in this fog, thinks we're sheep rustlers and shoots us in the gut," Max offered, less optimistically.

"Listen, Nancy Negative," Commander Joe groused, "unless you've got a better idea, keep your trap shut and your chin up. I vote for finding us a shepherd."

"Let's go," Newton said. "I think the bleating came from this way."

The fog had thickened. Every couple of minutes the group would stop, listen for baaing and hazard a guess as to the direction. Newton worried that the fog made the voices ricochet unpredictably and that they would never find the animals. However, he reasoned that being in motion at least kept them warm.

Max complained the entire time, and Newton had no choice but to ignore him. International travel had transformed the kid into a two-year-old in tantrum mode. If Max weren't Newton's best friend, Newton might have abandoned him on the mountains, leaving him to find his own way home.

After hours of tromping they finally honed in on the bleating. They were definitely getting closer. Max was the first to find the herd, tripping over a sleeping sheep and landed, face first, in manure. "Help me!" he demanded. He stood up, poo plastered all over him.

Newton rushed over to see if he could make the situation better, and as he did he smelled something close by: meat roasting. While he was wiping the filth from Max's face, he felt something cold on the back of his neck.

"Make one move, Shorty, and I'll use this shotgun to clean your ears out," a woman's voice declared. The tone was not the least bit friendly.

Max, his eyelids now poo-free, said, "It's the smelly sheep lady and she's got a gun, Newton."

"Smelly!" Jerry O'Brien's granddaughter declared, obviously offended, now pointing the gun at Max. "Who you calling smelly? I just took a bath last month."

Perhaps it was the cold, perhaps the altitude, perhaps the first-time experience of having a gun pointed at him, but Max fainted. His knees buckled and he fell to the ground, again face first in dung.

Jerry O'Brien's granddaughter turned to Newton. "What's his problem?" she asked. Max was not moving.

"He's got a lot of problems, but right now, I'd say mostly he's homesick. Truth be told, I think my friend misses his mother more than he thought he would. She's a really, really great mom."

This seemed to soften the shepherdess almost immediately. "Misses his mom! Ach, the poor thing. I miss me mom something fierce too." With that, Jerry O'Brien's granddaughter bent down and picked up Max like a baby, cradling him in her arms—though Max was much too big to be cradled. The effort caused her to let rip an enormous fart—a noise so loud that it sent shockwaves up the mountain. Jerry O'Brien's granddaughter acted as if nothing out of the ordinary had happened and carried Max through the herd of sheep, her head held high.

Commander Joe popped out of Newton's shirt. "Gas-mask time or what! Hurry up, Pokey, follow her or we might never see Max again."

Though the trail rose sharply, it wasn't long before they veered off and slipped through a moss-covered rock opening to a small enclosure. It was one of the most peaceful places Newton had ever been. Sound was muted, and it seemed church-like. The sanctuary was not quite a cave but was surrounded with stone, and the shepherdess had rigged up a crude tent as a shelter. She lay Max on a metal cot. By now he had woken up but was still groggy.

"Is this the end, Newton?" he asked. "Because if it is, I just want to say, coming to Ireland was the biggest mistake of my life."

Jerry O'Brien's granddaughter turned back toward Max. "Come again? What was that?" she asked, this time any trace of tenderness gone. There was a hardness to the question that made the rocks seem warm and fuzzy by comparison. Unfortunately Max was still too out of it to notice.

"This stinks," Max continued. "I've never been so miserable in my entire life. Honestly, who in their right mind would want to come to Ireland? It's cold and wet and smells like an outhouse."

Grabbing Max faster than a leg trap closing on a bear paw, Jerry O'Brien's granddaughter pinned him against a rock. "Listen, you wee whining son of a bog heap, Ireland is the greatest country on God's green earth. As for the outhouse comment, I've always carried an odour. That's my cross to bear, but if you have a problem with it, I'll throw you to the Leprechauns." She paused and sniffed the air. "Speaking of outhouses . . ."

Max managed to look terrified and embarrassed at the same time. Newton inwardly groaned.

Commander Joe whispered in his ear, "I'm not sure if Max is actually soldier material. So far his performance in the field has not been entirely successful."

Jerry O'Brien's granddaughter let go of Max. "There's a waterfall around the corner. Go clean yourself up." Max grabbed his knapsack and quickly took off without even looking at Newton or Joe. "So what about you two," the shepherdess asked, raising a fist. "Is there another country you're itching to visit, because as sure as sheep, I'll send you there right now, courtesy of my left and right fists."

Newton had no doubt that she would. "I adore Ireland. It's like one big four-leaf clover of charm. You'd have to be an idiot not to see its attractions. Besides, the Irish are the friendliest people on earth."

"You can say that again," the shepherdess agreed grumpily. She bent down and rotated the rabbit that was cooking on the fire.

"But I couldn't help being curious about something you mentioned when you were yelling at my friend," Newton continued. "Leprechauns?"

The rabbit dropped into the fire. Jerry O'Brien's granddaughter cursed as she retrieved it from the flames. "What about them?" she asked.

"I've heard that they live in Macgillycuddy's Reeks."

"They might."

"I need to find them."

"Leprechauns are foul, evil creatures. They are ruthless and cunning and greedy." Jerry O'Brien's granddaughter took the rabbit off the fire and brought it over to a chopping block. With one decisive swoop of the cleaver, the head came off cleanly. "You'd do best to forget about Leprechauns. Dinner's almost ready. Pull up a stool and we'll eat."

CHAPTER 6

The food seemed to cheer Max up somewhat. Newton thought roasted rabbit with beans never tasted so good. Surprisingly, even the dandelions were edible. The fact that the rain had stopped probably lightened the mood as well. Through the overhanging rocks they could see the clouds drift by, illuminated by the moon. Soon the fog had blown away and the stars shone brightly. Jerry O'Brien's granddaughter took out a pipe, lit it and poked at the fire. She stared at the flames for a long time before talking.

"Wool and manure is in our blood. For eons our family has lived on these mountains, tending sheep," she began. "My mother and father took over the flock after Grandpa retired to town. In fact, I was born on a wild night in the spot where we are sitting.

"Ma was the fairest, finest woman around, and my pa, well, let's just say he cut a rather splendid figure himself.

Together there wasn't a handsomer couple in all of Ireland," the shepherdess bragged.

Newton looked at the daughter and had an extremely hard time believing her parents were a fraction as dashing as she described. That or the gene pool had taken a dramatic hit in one generation. "As their only child, I felt like a princess. Growing up was a fairy tale. It was just me, Ma and Dad and our sheep." Jerry O'Brien's granddaughter paused and poked at the fire again. "That is, until the Leprechauns wrecked everything."

A tear rolled down her cheek and landed on the fire with a hiss. "I was still a wee thing, even younger than you lads. My parents, like most people in Ireland, were obsessed with the legend of the Leprechauns' gold. For centuries it's been rumoured that there exists a place in these hills where untold wealth is hidden away. Every year they would take our flocks deeper and deeper into the mountains, enchanted with the idea of finding the secret treasures.

"On my thirteenth birthday they finally discovered a place that they had only dared dream existed." By this time Jerry O'Brien's granddaughter's pipe had gone out. She tapped it against a rock and began cleaning it. She relit the pipe again, and then built up the fire.

Commander Joe, who was standing on Newton's shoulder, whispered in his ear, "You think she's going to say anything else?"

"I don't know," Newton replied.

"Don't know what?" Jerry O'Brien's granddaughter asked.

It was obvious that she couldn't see or hear Commander Joe. Newton didn't feel like explaining to her how his plastic pal was actually not a toy. "Nothing," he muttered. "So what happened to your parents?"

"I can't talk about it," the shepherdess replied sadly, and stared up at the sky, puffing her pipe.

Newton glanced at Max and shrugged. He didn't want to press, but . . .

"Please, it is against the rules," Max said.

"What's against the rules?"

"You have to finish. It's not fair to start a story and then stop like that."

Jerry O'Brien's granddaughter stood up. Perhaps it was the fire, but the red of her eyes seemed to match the red of her hair. "Not fair! I'll tell you what's not fair! Being left to fend for yourself because your parents snuck out in the middle of the night! And when you went to find them the next day, you discovered that their bodies had been left for dead with a note pinned to your mother's chest explaining their fate!" By this point the shepherdess was practically shouting. "So don't tell me what's against the rules!"

Newton was pretty sure she was crying as she stumbled out of the enclosure and into the night.

"I'm sorry," Max mumbled as she passed, but he got no response.

"So what do you think the note said?" Commander Joe asked.

"Why don't we forget about what the note said? Her parents were killed by Leprechauns. What else do we need to know? Let's go home," Max said.

Newton stood up. "We can't. She might be our only hope of saving Herbert and Gertrude."

With that, he went out to find Jerry O'Brien's grand-daughter.

She was cradling a lamb in her arms, sitting on a rock, definitely crying.

"I'm sorry about your parents," Newton said as gently as he could. "Max just wanted to hear the end of the story. He didn't mean to make you upset. And I don't either, but I'm going to ask you a favour. You see, the Leprechauns have kidnapped my friends and it's all my fault. We've come to Ireland to save them." Newton explained the journey they had undertaken to find Herbert and Gertrude.

"Mark my words, if you don't turn around in the morning, you'll end up as dead as my ma and pa. Here, look at this." Jerry O'Brien's granddaughter opened the front pocket on the bib of her overalls and handed a note to Newton. "Mind you be careful with that, though. I'll slice your ear off if there's so much as a rumple in that."

The note was smudged and creased and dirty from being carried around for so long. It was also definitely rumpled. Newton opened the waxen paper delicately, afraid that he might rip it. The script was ornate—done in the old-fashioned style. Whoever had written it had a flair for calligraphy.

Let this be a warning to anyone who trespasses on our sacred land.
They will have their heart ripped out by a Leprechaun hand.

Newton looked up from the note and swallowed. "Heart ripped out?"

Jerry O'Brien's granddaughter nodded solemnly. "I didn't want to mention that detail. It was awful. Bloody. Worse than a sheep after a rabid wolf attack."

"I'm sorry."

"Not half as sorry as I've been. But though I don't blame my ma and pa, over the years I've come to realize that it was greed that got them into so much trouble. Our life was wonderful—what difference would a few bars of gold have made?"

"Will you take us to the spot where you last saw your parents?"

"Doesn't getting your heart ripped out scare you at all, lad?"

The notion made his nose twitch and his ears burn and terrified him more than his brothers ever had. But Newton knew that if he turned around and forgot about Leprechauns, he would never sleep well again, because he had let his friends down. "Yeah, it scares me."

"And you're still going? Why?"

"I've got my reasons."

Jerry O'Brien's granddaughter put down the sheep and came over to eyeball Newton. "You're an odd-looking boy and strange to boot. But I've done my duty and tried to warn you away from the Leprechauns. Since I've failed, the least I can do is lead you to the entrance to their kingdom. As sure as mud is brown, you'd die of starvation wandering around these mountains before you ever found the spot, and I can't let that happen. We'll head out first thing in the morning. Be warned, though, I'll take you no farther than the entrance."

"Thank you very much—" Newton stopped. He realized he didn't even know the shepherdess's name.

"Mary."

"Makes sense," Newton replied. "Mary had a little lamb."

Mary O'Brien didn't even crack a smile. "I suspect the jokes won't be coming quite as easily tomorrow. Now go back to your friend and the fire. I want to be alone with me thoughts. I'll wake you up before sunrise."

Newton thought he had only been asleep for a few minutes when he found himself being nudged roughly on his shoulder by the toe of Mary's boot. "Wake up, lads! We've got to get going if we hope to make it there before nightfall."

"It still is nightfall," Max griped.

Newton had decided not to tell Max about hearts being ripped out. Instead he suggested that Mary leading them to the Leprechauns' land was the best bit of luck they could have hoped for.

After a couple of hours of walking in the semi-darkness, the day finally revealed itself to be fresh and green and, thankfully, rain-free. If they hadn't been on a collision course with Leprechauns, Newton felt, he might have enjoyed himself. After all, this was his first trip to Europe.

Theirs was an odd procession, with Mary in front, followed by Newton, with Commander Joe unnoticed in his pocket, and Max in single-file behind her, then the flock of sheep dutifully bringing up the rear. Midway through the

morning Max insisted he and Newton switch places because the lead sheep had taken to biting his butt—a practice that made Max yelp each time with surprise. Newton didn't have the same problem because Commander Joe hung off the back of his belt and whacked the sheep in the nose the first time he tried it. After that, the ram stuck to munching grass instead of munching . . . well, you know what.

By lunch both Newton's and Max's feet were a mess. The damp, combined with the hours of hiking, had brought out blisters.

"Can you get gangrene from blisters?" Max asked, lifting up a blood-soaked sock that he had painfully peeled off.

"Oh sure. Happens all the time to soldiers. Most likely you'll only end up with a wicked infection," Commander Joe offered. "I remember a soldier in the Great Toy War of '79 who lost a leg from a sliver that went unpulled."

"Thanks. That's a comfort," Newton said.

"I'm not sure I'll be able to put my shoe on again," Max complained. "My feet have swollen so much."

Mary, who had been herding up stray sheep, came over and examined Max's feet. "Tsk, tsk!" she muttered. "It's a shame children don't learn to go barefoot any more."

"Will I lose my feet?" Max asked.

"Not before I lose my mind," Mary shot back, and pulled out a Mason jar of ointment from a saddlebag strapped to one of her sheep. "This may hurt a bit," she said, and began applying the ointment. From Max's reaction, it appeared to hurt a lot! His screams sent some of the sheep scattering. Smoke rose from his feet and Newton wondered if Mary had mistakenly spread acid on them. However, when the smoke finally cleared, Max's feet were blister-free—like something out of a sci-fi movie.

Newton was amazed. There was no substance on earth that had those kinds of regenerative powers. "What is that stuff?" he asked.

Mary smiled slyly. "A secret formula that's as old as the mountains. I'll never tell. It's been passed down in my family for generations. Now give me your feet and I'll fix them too. If you'd be a dear and muffle the screams, I'd sure appreciate it. My sheep are already a little skittish about being on the move."

Soon after the break they left the open path and began cutting through narrow passageways in the rock that Newton was certain would lead to a dead end. However, Mary seemed to know where she was going. She picked out a route between the huge, moss-covered slabs of rock. The deeper they went, the less sky Newton could see. The enclosed space began to feel more and more like a coffin.

Only once did the passage open up for a brief few yards to reveal that their path was actually a narrow mountain ledge with a precipitous drop-off into a misty abyss with no visible bottom. By clinging to the wet rock and refusing to look down, Newton managed to edge his way along. A terrified Max whimpered across this section on his hands and knees, looking quite sheep-like.

"Pokey?" Commander Joe asked, as they waited for Max to crawl along the path. Mary had already gone ahead to scout the terrain. "How are we ever going to find our way back?"

Commander Joe must have been reading his mind. Newton was more turned around than a frog in a blender. Newton also wondered if Mary hadn't become a little disoriented herself. She seemed much less confident as the hours wore on. A couple of times Mary stopped at a fork in the path and appeared indecisive about which one to take. Was she completely lost but too proud to admit it? Newton dared not ask, as they continued trudging through these strange outcroppings. Though Newton was exhausted, the only possible hint of fatigue that Mary revealed was an increased crotchetiness and almost total lack of interest in conversation.

Night fell and still they continued their dreary journey, tired and hungry.

"We came on this mission woefully unprepared," Max said miserably. "I really don't know why you talked me into this."

"First rule of combat," Commander Joe said. "No complaining."

"That's a stupid rule," said Max.

"Maybe you're not military material," Joe shot back.

"Maybe you're—"

"Shh!" Mary warned Max sharply, putting her finger to her lips. "Stop blabbering to yourself. We're here."

Newton couldn't have been more surprised if Mary had said that peanut butter came from grapes. They were in the middle of yet another corridor of rocks, seemingly no different from the endless passages they had already gone through.

"Are you sure?" Newton asked, and for his curiosity received a sharp blow to the head from Mary.

"Of course I'm sure, you little ingrate. I know this place like I know the back of my sheep." Mary bent down and examined the ground. The shepherdess then took out her knife and scraped away at the moss until she uncovered a crude heart chiselled into rock. In the middle of the heart was the inscription *Jerry & Maggie R.I.P. Love, M.*

Mary bent over and kissed the tombstone, a lone tear falling to the ground. She got back up. "I've done all I can for you lads. May God protect your souls."

And with that, she turned and left.

Neither Newton nor Max was bold enough to ask Mary what they were supposed to do now. She seemed so sad, so within herself, that the question would have been inappropriate—like eating a spoonful of sugar right after brushing your teeth.

It wouldn't be long before they would regret their silence.

CHAPTER 7

"You boys must be hungry," Commander Joe said. They had been searching for some kind of opening in the rock face for over an hour, without any luck.

"If I had a little salt I'd consider eating my arm," Newton responded.

"Did she really abandon us, just like that?" Max asked, still looking forlornly toward the turn where Mary had disappeared. It was as if he expected her to come back at any moment.

Newton was becoming less and less certain that among the fissures and cervices there actually was an entrance to the Leprechaun kingdom.

"Leprechauns don't appear to throw out the welcome mat for visitors," Commander Joe said. "I mean, I can't even see a doorbell."

Newton looked around, trying to figure out a way into . . . what? A cave? A kingdom? A huge trap? There was absolutely nothing to indicate an entrance. The night was getting darker and colder by the minute.

Newton took out his headlamp and got on his hands and knees to examine the spot where Mary had once chiselled the heart. It revealed nothing. As he was staring at it, Newton was suddenly overcome with fatigue. He shook his head and tried to remain alert, but it was no use. He couldn't finish thoughts, let alone keep his eyelids open. Starvation no longer mattered. All Newton wanted to do . . . was . . . put . . . his . . . head . . . down . . . and . . . rest . . .

Newton opened his eyes. He had no idea how long he had been asleep. The small piece of sky that he could see through the opening revealed that night had fallen. Max and Commander Joe were also asleep.

What had happened? Why had they all passed out? Newton wondered if they had been exposed to sleeping gas. It didn't make sense that they all would have just conked out. They weren't *that* tired. Though he felt fine (aside from being wickedly hungry), Newton was worried that he had been exposed to some mind-altering chemical that had wiped out his brain cells responsible for inventing.

As Newton scanned the area with the weak beam of his headlamp, he thought he saw something twinkling high above them, near the top of the wall.

Because the walls were close together, Newton was able to shimmy up. When he was a couple of stories off the ground, he finally saw the source of the twinkling—a gold four-leaf clover. The clover was an exact replica of the one that Newton had picked up in his tree fort.

Normally Newton would have shied away from even touching the clover, but the circumstances were anything but normal. Even if it was a homing device, at this point, he had nothing to lose. As soon as he tried to pry it off the wall, the rocks began to rumble and press slowly together. It was as if he had angered the mountain. Newton scrambled back down to the ground.

"Wake up, Max! Wake up, Commander Joe!" Newton shouted. His two friends looked around groggily. As the walls inched even closer, Newton tried to figure out an escape route. Time was short.

"Come on, Pokey and Max! This way!" Commander Joe yelled, now fully awake. They sprinted in the direction that they had come from, but were forced to stop when a stone wall suddenly rose from the ground, blocking their way. Turning around, they saw that a fourth wall had risen up.

They were trapped.

The walls continued to move in. Newton scooped up Joe and put him in his chest pocket.

"If this is our last goodbye, by all means, let's go down like men!" Commander Joe shouted.

Max started blubbering. "I don't want to die!"

The walls inched ever closer together. Newton and Max were forced to turn sideways. The ends to the tunnel were also advancing inward. Surely in seconds they would be squished into sausages. The only thing Newton kept thinking was, I won't live to perfect the time machine. Strangely, his life didn't flash before his eyes.

He grabbed Max's hand. "I'm sorry about all this, Max. I never should have asked you to come along."

Max looked terrified. "I made my own choices, Newton. You have nothing to apologize for. Thanks for putting up with me for so long. I know I haven't been the easiest person to get along with." It was incredible that at the height of danger, Max wasn't panicking.

Newton could feel the rock against his nose. He turned his head to give himself a few more moments of life. Max had also turned his head, and now they were looking directly at each other.

"You've been a great best friend," Newton said sincerely. Somehow it was easier knowing that Max did not blame Newton for the fact that he was going to die at such a young age.

"You too, Newton. You're definitely one of a kind."

"What about me, Pokey?" Commander Joe shouted, though his voice was muffled.

"For a mass-produced toy, you've also managed to become one of a kind!"

The walls pressed against his ears. Newton now knew what it felt like to be in a vice. Would his head crack open like a nut, or would there be more of a mushy sensation? Newton saw Max scrunch his eyes shut and decided to do the same thing. After all, it would probably be some kind of bad luck to have as your last image your friend's brains getting splattered all over the place.

At the last moment, before squishification was about to occur, the ground opened up like a trap door and, suddenly, Newton, Max and Commander Joe were hurtling down a huge grass slide. Though the ride was slightly uncomfortable—it felt like one long slide into first base—it was much less so than than human pulverization. When they finally stopped, beside the bluest river Newton had ever seen, the trio were dazed but unhurt. Grass stains covered their clothes.

"We're alive!" Newton shouted.

Max looked at his pants and a smile spread across his face. "Hey! The most terrifying moment of my life and I don't need another new pair of underwear!"

Newton was amazed at Max's attitude. Miracle of miracles, he wasn't whining or blaming Newton for almost getting him killed. He was smiling!

"You did well, men," Commander Joe commended. "I've seen professional soldiers go to pieces under less stressful situations. You should be proud of your conduct. A word of caution, however, before we start handing out medals for valour. We better get a read on the situation ASAP. From now on, never forget, we've officially crossed into enemy territory."

Commander Joe was right. As much as Newton was savouring the fact that they were alive, he knew that this might be a very, very temporary situation. He remembered Mary's story about her parents' hearts getting ripped out. The only problem was, he couldn't figure out where danger might be lurking. Newton expected the river water to be cold, but when he scooped up a handful, it felt almost tropical. The river snaked through a valley that was so green it could have come from a movie set. The air was warm and didn't carry any trace of dampness from the rock passages. It was as if they had emerged into an entirely different world.

Newton fished out the page from *A History of Ireland: The Unauthorized Version* and read aloud:

Drop into a valley that hase no name
That doesn't exist but is there all the same.

They had "dropped" into the valley just as the verse directed.

Meanwhile Max was scanning the valley with his binoculars. "So what's the plan? If the instructions up to now were vague, that last part is a complete mystery. Would it have killed them to include a map?"

"Did you ever think that maybe these guys aren't exactly interested in having the tour buses come around taking pictures?" Joe said testily.

Newton thought that Max had a valid point. The valley seemed uninhabited, and he had no idea where to go. Food, or lack of it, was another issue that would soon need attention.

"Okay," Newton announced. "To find Leprechauns, we need to start thinking like Leprechauns. So, if I were a Leprechaun, where would I hide my gold? Once we figure that out, we'll find our foes, and hopefully then, we'll find our friends."

"Or we could just see if there are Leprechauns near where that smoke is," Max suggested, putting down his binoculars.

"What smoke?" Newton asked.

Max handed him his binoculars. "Over there."

Newton peered through the lenses. He had forgotten

that Max's dad, an avid birder, owned a world-class pair of German-made field glasses. Down in the valley he could see a plume of dark smoke rising from a thicket of trees.

"Good work, Max."

"I suggest we camouflage ourselves," Commander Joe said.

"With what? Grass?" Max asked.

"Excellent idea. Now you're thinking like a real soldier."

Max shook his head. "I was actually kidding. What are we going to use to attach the grass? Do you have a glue gun?"

"In that case, we crawl."

"Is your plastic melting?" Newton asked incredulously. "It would take us all day."

Commander Joe bridled. "Easy, soldier, there are no wrong ideas in the combat field. We want to maintain the element of surprise."

Surprise or no surprise, after a brief debate, they agreed that they had no other option but to walk toward the source of the smoke.

The sun had come up, the day was hot and Newton was dizzy from lack of food and water. After an hour spent beelining toward the smoke, they were beside the river again but appeared no closer to their destination. Newton's canteen was empty, his tongue was sandpaper and his eyelids were baked. He stared at his reflection in the glass-smooth river.

"Do you think this is safe to drink?"

Commander Joe peered into the river. "I'd be careful. Maybe the water has been poisoned. I wouldn't put it past the enemy."

Max was obviously as thirsty as Newton. "I'll take my chances." He began scooping water and drinking greedily.

When he didn't instantly die, Newton joined him.

Forty-five minutes later they finally veered from the riverbank and started walking along a narrow path that cut through a grove of pine trees. The ground was covered with needles and dust kicked up and reminded Newton of his pine tree at home. As they got closer to the source of the smoke they could smell something awful burning.

An opening in the trees revealed a furnace-like contraption with a high, black chimney spewing out foul smoke. Mere feet away from the furnace, a soot-covered Troll, with two tusks that looked like they could easily gore a person, was snoring. Beside him was a large box, made entirely of steel.

The trio hadn't even had time to figure out a plan when the Troll sprang to his feet, brandishing a trident. He sniffed the air suspiciously, then wailed, "Get away from me! It's not the end of the month!"

Newton stepped forward. "We're not who you think—" He couldn't finish the sentence because the Troll swung the three-pronged weapon at him with menacing force. If Newton had been a fraction of a second later in ducking, the blow would have been lethal. He backed up. "Easy, there. Easy."

The Troll swung again, but this time he came nowhere near them. "Go away! They're not ready yet!"

Max shouted, "We're not Leprechauns!"

The Troll momentarily stopped swinging, his spear poised above his head. "Liars! Nobody else lives in this valley!"

"Do we look like Leprechauns?" Max asked.

The question seemed to catch the Troll off guard. He appeared unsure how to answer. "I don't know . . ."

"Either we look like Leprechauns or we don't," Max said, surprisingly impatient with the large, irate, most likely extremely dangerous creature.

"Well . . . I don't know. You see . . . I'm blind," the Troll finally admitted, and opened his eyelids to reveal sockets that lacked eyeballs. A fairly disgusting deformity that Newton would have felt rude staring at, except, well, the Troll was blind.

This confession seemed to take some of the wind out of Max's sails. "Have you always been blind?"

"No."

"Then, do you remember what Leprechauns look like?"

"Of course. Once you see the greedy little creatures, you don't easily forget their sharp noses or pointy ears."

"Well, here's the deal then: if you promise not to kill me, I'll let you feel my face. I'm pretty sure that after that, you'll agree I'm not a Leprechaun."

"How do I know you're not going to trick me?"

"How do I know you're going to keep your word and not gore me?" Max retorted matter-of-factly. "I don't. So I guess we'll just have to trust each other, now, won't we."

Newton was amazed at Max's bravery, impressed that he was unafraid to battle wits with a creature that might be deadly. What had happened to Newton's best friend? Why wasn't he terrified?

Max boldly walked toward the Troll. As he got closer, the Troll sniffed the air more vigorously.

"Well, at least you don't have that obnoxious minty Leprechaun smell," the Troll said nervously, pawing at the air above Max's head. Max grabbed the Troll's hand, but the beast pulled it back like it had been burned with hot coals. "What are you doing?" the Troll roared.

Commander Joe covered his eyes. "I don't like the looks of this one bit, Pokey. Your friend seems to have a death wish."

Max didn't even flinch. "Where's that trust we were talking about?" he demanded. "Now relax, and please stop freaking out. It's making all of us nervous. I'm going to put your hand on my face."

When Max grabbed the Troll's hand again, Newton could see that it took all of the creature's willpower not to pull it back.

Max directed the huge hand toward his face. "Feel for yourself, but don't get too frisky, I'm susceptible to rashes," Max said.

The Troll felt Max's face delicately. For such an ugly, ungainly, lumbering creature, his hands had the dexterity of a concert pianist's. After the examination was complete, the creature broke into an ugly smile.

"Hey, you're actually not a Leprechaun!" he exclaimed. But the smile left his face as quickly as it had appeared. "What about your friends? Let me give them the face-test too."

Once the Troll was certain that the group was Leprechaun-free, he relaxed considerably (after getting over his amazement at Joe's size). "I'm Simon," he declared. "It's been a long time since I met someone who wasn't hell-bent on tormenting me."

"You wouldn't happen to have any food around here, would you, Simon?" Commander Joe asked once the pleasantries had been exchanged. "Me, I don't have a stomach, so I'm fine, but I've got two foot soldiers that are going to start eating dirt pretty soon—they're that hungry."

Simon, being a Troll, had no trouble hearing Commander

Joe; obviously he had a fully intact imagination. "Food? Of course. I've got more food than I know what to do with." Simon turned, brushed dirt away and uncovered a metal handle. He lifted a door that led into a cellar. "Come along. Let's get you fellows out of sight for a while."

Newton looked at Max and shrugged. What did they have to lose? If Simon was a kid-eating Troll and leading them into a trap, was it really much worse than starving to death?

The cellar was damp and very cramped. Old rags were scattered around the floor, but not much else. Of course there wasn't any light, so they used their headlamps. Because Simon buried his food in a hole, the flatbread and onions were covered in a fine layer of dirt. In spite of Newton's ferocious hunger, he shivered each time his molars crunched grit.

Nonetheless, they tore into the food. As they ate, Simon told them how the valley had once been filled with both Trolls and Leprechauns—both races known for their gentle natures. They had lived together peacefully for centuries—until the arrival of two particular Leprechauns, Michael O'Leary and his wife, Molly, ninety-two years earlier. "No one knew where they came from. I suspect that they may have been raised by the devil himself, they were that nasty. Before anyone could say 'Top of the mornin' to you!' the O'Learys had wrested control of the Leprechaun nation from the existing leaders.

"Now don't get me wrong, Leprechauns always had a soft spot in their hearts for gold, but Michael and Molly soon turned this into an obsession. In short order, hoarding the precious metal was the only thing their greedy hearts cared about. The entire kingdom had been brainwashed into believing the world's entire supply of gold belonged to them. Every last flake," Simon informed them.

"But what does that have to do with Trolls?" Max asked.

"They stole all our gold," Simon said sadly. "And in doing so, killed every Troll in the valley."

"How could they do that?" Newton asked. "Surely Trolls would crush Leprechauns." Simon was at least four times as big as the Leprechauns that had chased Newton through the night.

"Size has nothing to do with it. Leprechauns are the world's best thieves. They could steal the air from your lungs. They can sneak in anywhere undetected. More importantly, from a mile away, they can sniff out a flake of gold lying at the bottom of an outhouse."

Since his time machine was missing, Newton didn't doubt their skills.

Simon continued. "When a Troll is born in this valley, the first thing that happens is that a small gold nugget is placed in their tusks. Though the tusks grow around the flake, Trolls have always believed that the gold will protect them from disease. Unfortunately, the Leprechauns' lust for gold grew so strong that they snuck into our cellars one night and sawed off the tusks for these measly flakes. By the time everyone woke up in the morning, it was too late. They were beyond help."

"So gold really does protect them?" Max said.

"No. Or maybe. Who knows? It's not that Trolls can't survive without gold. They can't live without their tusks. It took almost a day of suffering, but by nightfall, every last Troll in the valley was dead. Except one."

A silence settled on the group. It was gently broken by Max. "But you still have your tusks?"

"Oh, lucky me. Simon is soooo fortunate—he just got his eyes poked out! " the Troll ranted.

"Did you hide or manage to escape?" Commander Joe asked.

"No. They left me alone because they needed me to make vaults for them."

"Make what?" Newton asked.

Simon pointed to the metal box next to him.

"Vaults? Those look like ordinary boxes to me," Newton said.

"Then looks are deceiving. This metal is so secure that nothing can penetrate it. The locks can be opened only by a magic spell. Trust me, there is not a safer place for Leprechauns to store their precious gold."

Newton examined the vault more closely and noticed an intricate series of gears, tumblers and pins. "But how do you manage? You're blind," he asked.

"Our race has metalworking in our blood. We were born to do this. You know, before I lost my eyes, I always believed I could blacksmith blindfolded. Of course, now I'm positive."

When Commander Joe asked why the Leprechauns didn't simply make the vaults themselves, Simon explained that they couldn't stand the smoke. "They're only into precious metals." As a result, the Troll was under strict orders to build a vault every two weeks in exchange for food. The one and only time he refused, the torture was too horrible to mention. Simon didn't dare refuse their demands again. "Trolls aren't meant to live alone. We need community. I miss my family. I miss my friends. Even after all these years it's not gotten any less lonely."

"Leprechauns sound like pure evil," Joe said.

Newton had never encountered a creature as sad as the Troll. "Couldn't you run away? So at least you'd be around other Trolls?"

Simon shook his head. "Where? How? I have no eyes. I've lived in this valley all my life. To be honest, I've never even ventured beyond these hills."

"Do you happen to know where we can find them?" Max asked.

"Find them! Haven't you listened to a word I've said? Run away from here as fast as you can."

Newton explained about Herbert and Gertrude.

"My guess is that your friends are dead by now," Simon said. "I mean, why would Leprechauns want to keep a couple of giants alive? It costs gold to feed them."

"They have to be alive," Newton insisted. "Or else the Merriwart kingdom is in big trouble. Could you please just give us directions?"

"No."

"Come on," Max insisted. "We won't tell them it was you who showed us the way. Honest."

The Troll shook his head firmly. "Forget it. Go home. I'd just be sending you to your deaths, and I couldn't live with myself knowing that. Besides, they'd figure out pretty quickly it was me. They may be short but they're not stupid."

"Okay. So if that's the way it's going to be," Commander Joe retorted, "then who needs your help? We'll find them ourselves!" With that, he turned and marched away.

Without pause, Max followed. Leaving Newton staring at the Troll.

"Well, I guess this is goodbye, Simon. Thanks for the food."

"Goodbye, Newton," Simon said, so woefully that Newton felt the back of his throat crunch up. "I am really sorry. Even if somehow you managed to sneak in, there's no way you'd ever find your way out again."

"To be totally honest, Simon, we're already way past that point. I don't have a clue where we are, much less how to get home. So what choice is there but to keep putting one foot in front of the other until I find my friends and get my invention back?"

Max and Joe had walked far enough ahead now that they were out of sight. Newton started after them. But he didn't get more than a few paces before Simon stopped him.

"Okay, I'll do it."

"Do what?" Newton asked.

"Sneak you into the Leprechauns' kingdom."

Newton smiled. "I knew you had it in you, Simon. That's the spirit."

"But you have to promise me one thing. If you somehow make it out alive, you've got to come back for me."

Newton promised. "Where do you want to go?"

Simon shook his head sadly. "Anywhere but here," he said. "Anywhere but here."

CHAPTER 8

Fortunately the Leprechauns were scheduled to pick up Simon's vault the next day. Otherwise Newton, Max and Commander Joe could have been waiting for days. Simon's plan was remarkably simple: hide inside the vault and simply let the Leprechauns hand-deliver them into the kingdom.

"I like a Trojan Horse as much as the next soldier," Commander Joe said, "but I've got some concerns." Simon assured Joe that Leprechauns would not open the vault until they got inside their kingdom. Why should they? The Troll had been making vaults for years—he was beyond suspicion.

As for Joe's other concern, how to open the vault from the inside, Simon customized a secret lock strictly for their use. He showed them how to press the button to open it. "Of course, you might not even need it if the Leprechauns decide to open the vault straightaway and start loading gold in it. My guess is it will be a quick death."

"Won't they notice the extra weight with us inside?" Max asked.

"Doubtful. A couple of extra kids won't make a difference. These vaults are made from high-density lead. You wouldn't know it to look at them but they weigh over two tonnes."

Newton was incredulous. The vaults weren't much bigger than a five-person tent; it seemed to defy logic that they could be that heavy.

They were jostled a bit as the vault was loaded onto what Newton assumed was some sort of cart. Inside, the vault was almost pitch dark except for two tiny air holes—pin-pricks really.

"At least there's more room in here than in the FedEx box," Newton whispered to Max.

"Do you think we're going to make it out of this alive, Newton?"

"Honestly, I don't know," Newton responded. Usually, with Max, he wouldn't dare mention the possibility of fail-ure. But ever since Max had survived almost getting crushed to death, he was different. Calmer. More certain of himself. "You okay with that?"

"Wouldn't miss it for the world. I think I might get a little shut-eye while I can." And Max, now apparently one cool customer, drifted off to sleep.

As they bumped along, Newton had time to try to think of a plan. Of course, without any idea what they were getting into, none came. Instead, he turned his mental attention to his time machine. Ever since the initial test run, Newton had been trying to figure out what was bothering him before he activated the countdown to send Gertrude and Herbert back three centuries. Something hadn't been right. Because Newton had invented it, he knew the machine intimately. It made no difference that physically it wasn't in front of him (or that it had been stolen). Mentally he started reviewing connections, circuit wiring, photoreceptors, motherboards, snaking through every circuit breaker in the machine, trying to pinpoint where he might have overlooked something.

The mental gymnastics of trying to find the glitch was tiring, and somewhere along the journey Newton fell asleep.

He was awoken when the vault got unloaded. The Leprechauns obviously just let go and dropped the vault off the cart, and it took everything Newton had not to scream in pain when he bashed his head. Newton's ears were ringing. Max groaned.

After a few minutes, all outside noises stopped. They couldn't hear anything. Joe whispered, "Well, soldiers, are you feeling lucky?"

"As a four-leaf clover," Max replied.

"Then let's do this," Newton said, and pressed the button to unlock the vault.

Nothing happened.

"Let's go, Newton," Commander Joe said. "What are you waiting for?"

"Something's not working," Newton replied, trying not to panic but still imagining the horrible end to their adventure if the lock didn't open. He tried again, this time pushing harder.

Still nothing. In the darkness Newton felt along the steel, searching for another button, anything to get them out of there.

"Hurry up, Newton, I have to pee," Max said. "And not because I'm nervous. I just really need to go."

The steel was smooth. There weren't any other indentations on the surface. Maybe Simon wasn't quite the locksmith he claimed to be. Without much hope, once more, Newton pushed the button, this time pressing so hard that he thought he might have double-jointed his index finger.

Thankfully his increased efforts finally released the lock. Cautiously Newton pushed the door open a crack and peered out. The room was bathed in a green light. "I don't see anyone," he whispered. Tucking Commander Joe in his front pocket, he crept out of the vault. Max followed.

As his eyes adjusted to the light, Newton realized that the room was huge—bigger than an indoor football stadium but much cozier—it had the rich, hushed quality of an old library. Row upon row of shelving stretched from floor to ceiling. Except, instead of books on the shelves, there were hundreds, maybe thousands of vaults, exactly like the one from which they had just emerged. Stepladders that slid across the rows were obviously used to climb to the higher levels.

"This is incredible," Max said, his mouth open in awe. "Do you think all these vaults are filled with gold?"

"Well, it most likely isn't peanut butter. Keep moving, soldiers," Commander Joe ordered.

"Do you realize that we're probably walking between billions of dollars' worth of gold?" Newton said. It was staggering to try to comprehend that kind of wealth.

"Actually more like three gazillion, eight trillion, two hundred and twelve billion, sixty-four million, ten thousand, three hundred and fourteen dollars' worth—give or take a few trillion depending on what gold is trading at," a voice spat out. "Hands up! Now!"

Newton turned and could see that the voice belonged to a Leprechaun brandishing an ancient rifle—a firearm that might have been state-of-the-art three hundred years ago. The little fellow came just to Newton's chest, but looked like he could chew metal.

He was not alone. Standing shoulder to shoulder, at least three deep, was a mob of Leprechauns, all wearing angry scowls and also brandishing rifles.

"This doesn't look good, Pokey," Joe whispered from Newton's pocket.

"March!" the Leprechaun ordered, and prodded Newton in the back toward a door at the far end of the building.

Max, who was beside him, looked at Newton, winked and gave a slight smile. Newton couldn't believe it. Max winking in the face of death? Somehow his best friend's show of bravery made Newton feel much better. Like maybe there was a chance they'd get out of this alive now that his plan of sneaking undetected into the Leprechauns' lair had completely backfired.

Newton was surprised to see the sun shining when they emerged from the gold storage building. He had envisioned an underground, gloomy, secretive world, but this was the opposite. The place was rather cheery. Under any other circumstances (namely, not fearing for his life), Newton would have described it as cute. Green-and-gold was the predominant colour scheme. It had an amusement park quality to it—the buildings seemed fake, like they were too perfect to be real. For a kid, the scale of this world was comforting. Everything was built for adults that were only three and a half feet tall. Houses looked medieval, most likely because of their thatched roofs. As they were paraded down the main street of town, Leprechauns came out of shops and houses to stare at them. Occasionally a Leprechaun would fly past on a broomstick, though most were on foot.

They made their way through a zigzag of narrow streets, under a midday sun, until they reached a large courtyard. In the centre of this square stood a wooden platform. A hangman's noose dangled from a beam, and in the noose was the neck of a very scared-looking Leprechaun. Only a smattering of Leprechauns were on hand to watch the proceedings. They seemed rather bored. Newton was riveted. Surely they weren't going to hang someone this casually? A hangman Leprechaun had his hand on a lever that Newton assumed worked the trap door on the scaffolding.

"Any last words, prisoner?" he asked.

"Just that I'm sorry," the green fellow said, almost crying.

The spectators laughed, and Newton caught some of their conversation "He was sorry! Imagine!" "Who cares?"

"Been there. Done it. Heard the sob story," the hangman replied far too jovially considering that the next moment he released the trap door. It took only a few seconds of twitching and convulsing before the Leprechaun's body was still.

"Not even a scream this time," one of his captures muttered, obviously disappointed.

"Oh well, you can't win them all," another replied.

Newton glanced at Max. His friend looked like he was doing his best not to throw up.

As they continued through the courtyard, Newton saw that the one end was dominated by a castle that dwarfed every other structure around it. The turrets seemed to rise up to the sky and the gold bricks shone brilliantly. Newton had never seen anything so beautiful, and would have noticed it much earlier, but his attention had been understandably diverted. As they approached, the drawbridge came down and two sentries nodded to the mob that had escorted Newton, Max and Commander Joe.

"We'll take it from here," the larger of the two sentries barked, and roughly shoved the prisoners through the arched entranceway.

The castle's main hallway looked to be painted with real gold and to go on forever. About fifty paces in, they turned left and ducked through an arched doorway that opened to a small room, where a freight elevator waited. Again, they were roughly pushed inside. The door to the metal cage was slammed shut.

The elevator jolted dramatically before starting its downward journey. It felt like they were descending into a mineshaft.

Commander Joe was the first to break the silence. "Me, I'm not worried, my neck's way too small, but did you see that hangman's noose back there?"

"It was pretty hard to miss," Max replied. "Newton, please tell me you have a plan."

"Sorry. Not yet. My brain's still trying to process our

capture. I mean it was almost as if the Leprechauns were expecting our arrival."

"Yeah, I had that same sneaking suspicion," Joe agreed. "So where does that leave us?"

At that moment the elevator stopped abruptly and the cage automatically opened.

"In the dungeon," said an extremely fat, foul-smelling Leprechaun. "The place where criminals are dying to get out!" He laughed a vicious laugh. "Follow me."

They walked past a long row of cells. Leprechauns slept or sat slumped, not even raising their heads to watch the prisoners pass. Newton wondered if they were indeed dead. He wouldn't have been surprised considering the stench of the place. Newton kept hoping to see Herbert and Gertrude, but didn't.

The guard opened a cell. "In here," he said.

"Any idea how long before we're put on trial?" Max asked.

The guard laughed again. That laugh was starting to annoy Newton.

"Trial? What for? You're guilty. You'll be taken out tomorrow and hanged. Noon sharp. We haven't hanged a human in years. The whole kingdom is bound to turn up." The Leprechaun slammed the door shut, leaving two boys and one plastic action figure to ponder their fate.

"These guys don't fool around, do they," Max said.

"Apparently not," Commander Joe replied. "We're in deep, fellows. Reminds me of the time our platoon mistakenly parachuted into the middle of an elephant stampede. It was pachyderm pandemonium. A hopeless situation. There was no way out."

"What happened?" Newton asked.

"I was lucky. Just a few glancing blows. The rest of my comrades . . . well, let's hope our predicament turns out much better. They were good, good action figures who didn't deserve to die like that," Commander Joe lamented, and hung his head sadly.

"That story sucked," Max finally said. "We need some hope around here, not doom and gloom."

"You're absolutely right, soldier," Commander Joe replied. "Apologies all around. But that still doesn't change the fact that we're up to our eyeballs in cow dung without a shovel."

Eyeballs! That's it! Newton knew what his machine was missing. He had forgotten to solder the iris cap on the conductor coil of his invention. "I've got it!" he announced.

"You've figured out how to get us out of here?" Max asked hopefully.

"No. I just realized why my time machine didn't work."

"That's great, Newton, I'm really happy for you. But unfortunately, we'll all be dead before you can find out if you're right."

Newton ignored Max's comment and started banging on the metal bars. "Hey! Let us out of here! Hey! Mr. Leprechaun! I need to get out! NOW!"

Moments later the dungeon master was in front of their cell. "SHUT IT! Prisoners aren't allowed to talk, MUCH LESS YELL!" he shouted.

"Sorry," Newton replied. "I was not aware of that policy. I need to talk to Michael O'Leary right now."

The guard whacked the bars of the cell with his baton,

nearly crushing Newton's fingers. "No one talks to Michael O'Leary. Especially not prisoners. Not here. Not up there. Not anywhere. Besides, you're in no position to be telling anyone anything." The guard turned and started walking away.

"I repeat, I need to speak with Michael O'Leary," Newton said much more firmly (though inside he was quaking). "Tell him I know how to fix his time machine."

"What time machine?" the guard asked, not quite so belligerently.

"None of your business," Newton replied. "Do it!"

"Watch your tone, mister. I'm warning you." For a second the guard looked like he might reach into the cell and rip Newton's heart out. Instead he breathed in deeply, trying to control himself. "What if I think you're bluffing?"

"Fine. But I promise you this: just before I'm executed I'm going to announce to the crowd that I came all the way to your kingdom not to steal gold, but to fix the time machine, a machine that your leader, Michael O'Leary, knows will increase the Leprechaun fortunes more than a pea-brained fool like you could ever imagine. Then I'll inform everyone that you wouldn't listen to me." Newton paused, then added dramatically. "So I dare you, don't tell him."

The guard stared at Newton, trying to make him turn away. Instead Newton narrowed his eyes and glared right back, giving as good as he got, until the guard blinked and walked away without another word.

When he was out of earshot, Commander Joe whispered,

"I'm impressed, Pokey. That was an Oscar-worthy performance."

"Do you think he bought it?" Max asked.

"Let's hope so," Newton replied. "If he didn't, the game's
up. We're dead."

CHAPTER 9

By Newton's calculations it had been two days since they left home. Hours had passed in the cell with no food, no water and most importantly no word from the guard. He had not returned, and except for an occasional moan from a listless Leprechaun, the dungeon was eerily quiet. So quiet that Newton was beginning to think awfully grim thoughts. He wondered what it would feel like to walk up the platform, knowing your death was only moments away. Would he be brave, or would he bawl like a baby? Would he even be able to walk, or would his legs be so weak with fear that the Leprechauns would have to carry him to the noose?

Much later, Newton heard a door opening. The guard had returned, escorted by four more Leprechauns. "Okay, you come with me. Your friend stays," the guard ordered, indicating Max. He didn't know about Commander Joe.

"I don't think so," Newton replied much more calmly than he felt. "He's my assistant. My wingman. The only one

I can completely trust not to make a mistake and blow the machine to smithereens. Unless you can cough up a competent Leprechaun, schooled in the nuances of time machinery, he comes. If not, I might as well stay here."

The guard looked torn. Clearly he was under orders to bring just Newton. He mumbled to himself. Finally he looked up and said, "All right. But I don't understand why you didn't tell me this before."

"Because you never asked," Newton replied matter-of-factly.

Max was taking deep breaths, trying to stay calm. Newton could have sworn his knees were quaking.

For that comment the guard smacked Newton across the head. It hurt. Newton decided that the tactic of pretending he was a tough guy had reached its limit and he would be much more careful from here on out.

Michael O'Leary sat on a high gold throne. For someone so green, he wore an awfully black scowl. His wife Molly sat on a similar throne next to him with a pinched nose and red, glaring eyes. They stared ferociously down at Newton and Max. "YOU WHAT?" O'Leary sputtered. "HOW DARE YOU!"

"Then you might as well kill us now, sir," Newton replied. "I don't mean to cause any problems, but I need to see Herbert and Gertrude before I fix the machine."

"YOU ARE NOT IN A POSITION TO BE DEMANDING ANYTHING!" O'Leary screamed. It was amazing to watch how quickly he was losing it. The little fellow was freaking out, even though Newton was trying very hard to be polite.

Newton's demands had been simple. If he fixed the time machine, the Leprechauns would let them go—including Herbert and Gertrude. The only problem was that Newton didn't trust Michael O'Leary, and so before he set to work, he needed to confirm that the giants hadn't already been hanged. Newton tried again. "I realize that, but—"

"NO BUTS! YOU WILL DO AS I SAY!"

Commander Joe, who was still tucked in Newton's shirt, said, "This guy is a total nut-job, Pokey. Maybe you should try to calm him down instead of making him angrier."

"I'm doing the best I can, honest!" Newton whispered back. He really didn't know how to handle Michael O'Leary. The Leprechaun was a spewing volcano of anger, set to erupt at the slightest provocation. And yet, Newton was certain that unless he reunited with Herbert and Gertrude before he fixed the machine, he would never see them again. His plan depended on it.

"Okay, I'm sorry to have wasted your time. If you feel that way, we might as well be sent back to the dungeon," Newton declared with finality. "Thanks for at least agreeing to meet with us." Newton glanced over at Max, who was blinking in disbelief. He hated to put it on the line like this, but a lifetime of being bullied by his brothers made Newton understand that showing any sign of weakness or doubt would have serious consequences. It had to be all or nothing.

Molly O'Leary was the first to speak. "Hang them right now. They don't deserve the dungeon. I want them dead before lunch!"

Max fainted (clearly his new-found bravery had reached its limit), and Newton felt the blood rush from his face. What time was lunch?

The guards pressed in closer. "Let's go," one said gruffly. "To the noose with the lot of you," added another, as Newton was pushed and Max was lifted out of the court.

They were almost at the door when Michael O'Leary shrilly shouted, "STOP!" He took a deep breath. "Bring them to the workshop. If the kid is bluffing, he dies. If not, what do we have to lose? Our best engineers have had no luck fixing the machine." Though Newton's heart was still beating so fast he wouldn't have been surprised if his nose started gushing as a pressure release, the order allowed him to start breathing again.

"Thanks," Newton replied hoarsely.

Max opened his eyes and asked, "What happened?"

"You have exactly three hours," said Michael O'Leary. "If the machine is not working by then, start praying."

Three hours! What if the Leprechauns had irreparably damaged his invention? Tried to disassemble it in an effort to understand the complicated inner workings and not put it back together properly? Just undoing their mistakes might take days. However, the scowl on Michael O'Leary's face suggested that attempting to bargain would have dire consequences.

Led by Michael and Molly, they entered the workshop. The walls were made of stone and the ceiling was low and arched. Newton could touch it with his arms outstretched. It was quickly evident that the sole purpose of this place was to improve the thieving arts. Various safes were scattered about and blindfolded Leprechauns were in the process of trying to pick them. Alarm systems were being dismantled, tunnel-digging equipment was being tested out, bolt cutters that could cut through steel bars as thick as Newton's leg were being demonstrated. One section of the workshop was dedicated to sophisticated surveillance equipment—fantastical periscopes, spy-cameras that were attached to ladybug antennas and homing devices embedded in bubble gum. Under different circumstances he would have loved nosing around, checking out the ingenious devices. But now his interest was in only one thing—his time machine.

When he saw it resting on a bench, Newton couldn't help himself—he smiled. The machine appeared to be in one piece. Just being near it made Newton realize how much he had missed it, even though it had turned out to be the source of so much trouble. He rubbed his hand along the smooth surface and then glanced up to the six Leprechauns standing on the other side of the workbench. They were all wearing lab coats and, though they were green, had a scientific look to them.

"Where are Herbert and Gertrude?" Newton asked.

Michael O'Leary nodded. No sooner had a scientist pushed a button than a shelf containing beakers and scales flipped up and out stumbled the two Merriwart giants, blinking like they hadn't seen much light lately. They had to bend over to avoid hitting their heads on the ceiling.

"Newton!" Herbert gushed.

"I knew you'd find us!" Gertrude exclaimed.

Newton was relieved to discover that they were still alive. Unfortunately, in their excitement they forgot that their hands and feet were tied up. Before he went two steps, Herbert bashed his head on an overhead light, staggered backward and crashed into a shelf of beakers. Blood trickled down his forehead. Gertrude didn't fare much better. She tripped over a workbench and narrowly avoided crushing the time machine. Max lunged and slid it out of the way just in time. Because they were giants in a miniature world of Leprechauns, Gertrude and Herbert's natural clumsiness under the best of circumstances was positively lethal in the lab's cramped confines.

"Are you all right?" Newton asked.

"Oh, that was nothing," Herbert explained. "I've had worse accidents brushing my teeth."

Newton was surprised. In a million years he never would have guessed a toothbrush had come within ten feet of Herbert's chompers. In fact, Newton often wondered if the giant's teeth had moss growing on them.

"No, I mean your capture. Have they treated you well?"

"It's been a rather grand adventure" Gertrude replied. "For Herbie and me to be forced into such cramped quarters—let's just say it wasn't the worst thing in the world for a couple of lovebirds like us. If you know what I mean."

Newton could have sworn even the Leprechauns turned red with embarrassment.

"Gross," Max uttered.

"Newlyweds," Commander Joe spat in disgust.

Herbert tried to stand, and in the process knocked over more beakers.

"Don't make another move," Molly O'Leary hissed to Herbert. "The same goes for the fright queen beside you."

"Get them out of here before they cause any more damage," ordered Michael O'Leary.

"The giants stay," Newton replied calmly. "No offence, but I don't trust you."

"Fine. Have it your way. But if you can't fix this thing, we won't hang you," O'Leary declared.

"You won't?" Max asked hopefully.

"No, we'll torture you instead. Slowly and painfully, so that by the end of the ordeal you'll be begging us to kill you quickly."

This prompted Max to inch even closer to Newton.

"For the next little while I'll need you to remain quiet. This is going to take everything I've got. But pretend you're doing something very important," Newton whispered to Max.

"No problemo. I'm cool," Max responded.

"What about my brainpower, Pokey?" Commander Joe asked.

"Ditto. Eventually I'm going to need more hands, but until that time, if I have any hope of pulling this off, complete silence please."

"Roger. Over and out. My lips are zipped." Joe disappeared under the flap and into the front pocket of Newton's shirt.

Newton spoke to the Leprechaun scientists, who until that point hadn't moved. Maybe they were as scared of Molly and Michael as he was. "I'll need a soldering gun, a Number 2 Phillips screwdriver, an adjustable wrench and a spool of copper wiring."

Michael O'Leary was practically seething. "You do understand that that stuff costs money."

Newton couldn't believe what a cheapskate this guy was. Fortunately he remembered he had some money in his jeans. He fished out ten dollars. "Here. Keep the change."

It was the first time Michael had looked anything but angry. He nodded. Instantly the necessary materials were placed on the workbench.

Newton took a few deep breaths and tried to clear his mind. It was imperative that he mentally reconnect with his time machine. Even though he had had a eureka moment back in the dungeon when he figured out why his invention didn't work, he knew fixing it would be an incredibly delicate operation. The problem was that the conductor coil— the heart of the machine, but buried under layers of circuitry—was missing its iris cap. Newton had simply forgotten to put it in and never thought about it again—until he was in the dungeon.

He picked up the screwdriver and started removing circuitry panels. The lab Leprechauns leaned in with fascination, monitoring his every move. Their minty breath wafted into his nostrils. "Stand back please, I need my space!" Newton ordered.

Grudgingly they moved away from him.

The first time he looked at his wristwatch, Newton was shocked to discover that an hour had passed and still he was a long way from the conductor coil. Newton forced himself to work much faster. No longer could he afford the slow, cautious approach. Instead his hands practically flew in and out of the machine, taking it apart with a recklessness that he knew might have serious ramifications later on.

After two hours, circuitry was strewn across the workbench and he confirmed that, indeed, the iris cap was lying beside the conductor coil instead of over it. Max was hopping nervously from one foot to the other. Newton grabbed the copper wire.

"Here Max, hold on to this end and feed it to me when I tell you." He turned to Joe. "Get the solder gun ready."

"Locked and loaded, Pokey," Joe declared.

Newton grabbed the iris cap. His hands were shaking, which was a problem considering his margin of error was basically zero.

"Ready, Max?"

"As ever," Max declared confidently.

Newton brought the gun in contact with the copper that Max held next to the conductor coil. Just before a glob of the liquefied metal dropped, Newton placed the iris cap against it. "Make sure the seal on this is complete," he told Max. "It won't work if there are any gaps." Working quickly, he continued to melt the copper and wind it around the cap in one continuous line. He had no time to marvel at his manual dexterity.

"You've got forty-five minutes left," Michael O'Leary said, as Newton put the soldering gun down and started to piece the time machine back together as fast as he could.

"Could you extend the deadline?" Newton pleaded.

"No. Not one second more," said Molly sourly. "We've wasted too much time on you already and I don't believe you have a clue what you're doing."

Newton was not surprised that the Leprechauns were proving to be as stingy with time as they were with money. However, with five minutes remaining, Newton had reassembled almost the entire machine and in fact didn't need extra time. What parts remained scattered on the table were more window-dressing, not affecting the operation of the invention. Newton sincerely hoped that the Leprechaun scientists wouldn't realize this. The next part of his plan depended on it.

Taking a deep breath, Newton dropped a metal container, hoping no one would suspect the move wasn't accidental. Screws and washers flew everywhere. "We're doomed!" Newton gasped. "Quick, everyone look around while I keep putting this together."

"Any Leprechaun that lends a hand will be boiled pink," Molly threatened. "That's a direct order!"

"I found a screw!" Herbert exclaimed.

"Me too!" added Gertrude.

While his friends were scrambling to retrieve the screws, Newton secretly initiated the countdown sequence.

"Bring everything over here, please," replied Newton

urgently, not even bothering to look up. "I'll need them soon."

"Twenty seconds left!" Molly announced, looking at her watch.

"Please give me more time," Newton begged. "I'm almost finished. I just need to figure out where these three pieces go. In an hour I'll have this machine up and running!"

"A deal's a deal," replied Michael. "Besides, I'm sure our able scientists will be able to clean up your work from here."

Smoke started rising from the machine.

"What's going on?" Molly demanded.

"I don't know," Newton replied. But of course, he did. The atomizer was firing up. In less than ten seconds Newton would find out whether his machine was going to work.

A whirring noise came from the machine, loud and high-pitched. Max glanced at Newton. He looked terrified. Newton winked at him.

Unfortunately Michael O'Leary saw Newton's wink. "It's a bluff!" he cried. "The machine works. They're trying to escape. Shut it down!" Only four seconds were left on the countdown.

"Everyone touch the machine!" Newton shouted. "Whatever you do, don't let go!"

Michael O'Leary jumped on Newton and Molly went for Max, trying to pull them away. The rest of the Leprechauns stood around, too dumbfounded to move. Newton could feel his fingers slipping off the machine, but he managed to cling to it despite the Leprechaun's efforts.

And then everything was a blur. Newton's body felt like it was being pressed as thin as paper and dunked in a vat of ice-water. Fortunately, this sensation lasted only a few moments. The vise grip that had a stranglehold on his lungs lifted.

Newton opened his eyes, half expecting still to be in the lab. He clearly wasn't. Was it true? Had he actually pulled it off?

"Wow!" Max gasped. "I . . . I . . . I . . ." He couldn't complete the sentence.

Drool pooled down Herbert's and Gertrude's chins as they took in their surroundings.

"Pokey's hit the big-time!" Commander Joe shouted.

The time machine had worked! Not only was Newton alive, but he had created the greatest invention of his life. One instant he was in the middle of the Leprechaun lair, the next, he was in a lush jungle three million years earlier.

The only downside . . .

Molly and Michael had tagged along for the ride. And by the looks on their faces, it was obvious that they weren't quite as excited about time travel as Newton and his friends.

CHAPTER 10

They had landed in a clearing in a jungle, surrounded by trees so big that even Herbert and Gertrude gaped up at them in awe. Vines grew everywhere and leaves as big as umbrellas hung off the branches. This was a tropical rain forest on steroids.

"Holy Jurassic Park, Newton," Max gasped. "You did it! Where are we?"

"In the Mesozoic Era. About 140 million years ago. That is, if my machine's calibrations were correct," Newton replied, still in shock that his invention had worked.

Herbert and Gertrude looked at each other in amazement. "You're one freakishly smart kid, Newton," Gertrude exclaimed. "I mean, some weird stuff must be going on in your head to figure these things out."

Newton blushed.

"Good work, Pokey. This puts you in the big leagues as far

as inventors are concerned. One day you might even be mentioned in the same breath as Thomas Edison."

"Don't be ridiculous," Molly said. "The kid got lucky."

"And he's going to get unlucky if he doesn't bring us back to our kingdom right now!" Michael demanded, stomping his feet.

"Or what are you going to do about it?" Herbert asked, towering over the Leprechauns. Though he was still tied up, the giant cast an intimidating figure.

Without warning, Michael kicked Herbert in the shin so hard that the giant crumpled to the ground. Newton wondered if he'd broken the bone.

"That's what we're going to do about it, you oversized moron."

Gertrude, loyal to Herbert to a fault, made the tactical mistake of trying to bash Michael over the head as payback. A karate chop to her calf from Molly had the Queen writhing in pain next to Herbert. The ruthlessness of these blows was staggering. Next, Newton wouldn't have been surprised to see the Leprechauns climb up and bite the giants' ears off.

"Now get us back to our kingdom," Michael ordered Newton. "Before I pluck your eyes out and feed them to a T. rex." Had he not seen first-hand what the Leprechauns had done to Simon the Troll, Newton might have been under the false impression that this was an idle threat. Perhaps even a Leprechaun figure of speech.

It was not.

Newton never had a chance to reprogram the machine, because an honest-to-goodness pterodactyl swooped down and plucked the time machine from between them. There was no advance notice. They never saw it coming. The bird was helicopter huge and the air displacement from its beating wings as it retreated almost knocked Newton over. The bird was terrifying, but also exhilarating.

For a moment Newton couldn't breathe. The implications of seeing a pterodactyl were enormous. *Dinosaurs irrefutably existed, and Newton had seen one!*

The thrill of this discovery was slightly offset by the fact that the dinosaur had stolen their only way home. The group watched in silent astonishment as the pterodactyl flapped up to a nest located high in a giant tree and deposited the time machine in it.

"Hey! That's our property! Bring it back here immediately!" Molly shouted.

Newton didn't want to say so, but he found it pretty ridiculous that she was claiming ownership of a machine that was already stolen. Fearing a karate chop, Newton didn't dare correct her about the time machine's rightful owner.

"That was one gi-normous bird," Commander Joe said.

"Look, there's another one!" said Gertrude. She was lying on the ground, still in pain from the kick.

"And another and another and another and another," confirmed Herbert. The sky was suddenly filled with a flock of pterodactyls. They circled overhead like vultures, and Newton realized that their appearance might not be accidental. He remembered reading about the feeding habits of these creatures—they were carnivores.

"Are you thinking what I'm thinking, Pokey?" Commander Joe asked.

"Yup," Newton gulped.

"What exactly are you two thinking?" Max asked, not taking his eyes off the sky.

"That we're in deep trouble," Newton told him. "Right now, to those birds, we look like dinner!"

A pterodactyl must have been a lip reader (or had supersonic hearing), because no sooner had Newton finished speaking than the bird nosedived for the group. It plummeted like a torpedo. About twenty feet from them, the creature opened its beak, as if to scoop up the entire group in one mouthful. Newton hated to see his life end this way.

Fortunately, the Leprechauns never flinched. Michael unleashed a ferocious punch that was timed to perfection. The force of the blow snapped the creature's beak as it skidded to a stop and hopped around in excruciating pain, cawing so loudly that Newton's ears hurt. Molly dealt with the next bird in a similar manner.

It took only two more pterodactyls to be chop-sueyed senseless before the rest of the flock decided to look for their next meal elsewhere.

Commander Joe, who knew a thing or two about combat, had never seen such an awesome display. "Hats off to you both!" he said admiringly. "Where'd you learn to punch like that? Do you do weights?"

The Leprechauns turned to Newton. Clearly they could not hear Joe. "Did you recently eat a big bowl of stupid?" Molly barked. "Because sending us back here might have been the dumbest mistake of your life! Did you think you'd actually get away with it?"

"You were going to kill us anyway," Newton retorted.

"So really, what did I have to lose?"

The Leprechauns said nothing to contradict this notion—confirming that Newton's theory was true.

"So Mr. Smarty Pants, exactly how do you propose to get us out of this mess?" Michael asked.

At that particular moment, Newton did not have an answer. His time machine was out of reach and he seriously doubted whether he'd get it back. As he was formulating a response the ground started shaking.

"What's going on?" Max asked.

"Feels like an earthquake, Pokey," Commander Joe declared. "Powerful. Too bad we don't have a Richter scale to get a reading. I'll bet it's a 7."

Gertrude and Herbert huddled together as the tremor intensified. Newton thought that the earth was about to split open. His teeth chattered. His knees banged together as he fell to the ground.

And then he saw it. A herd of brachiosaurus, numbering twenty or more, running through an opening in the jungle, snorting and kicking up mud. They were so big, so powerful, that Newton was awestruck. Sure, pterodactyls were pretty impressive if they were the only prehistoric creature you ever got to see, but compared to brachiosaurus, they were gerbils. These majestic beasts thundered by. It seemed impossible that such large animals could move so fast. The creatures didn't give the visitors so much as a sideways glance, but instead, with necks craned forward, kept barrelling toward a path on the other side of the clearing, as if locked in a footrace. Within seconds they were gone. Gradually, the ground stopped shaking.

"That was incredible! Not just one, but a whole herd of B-boys!" Max exclaimed.

Newton felt the same way. This was infinitely better than seeing a deer or eagle out in the wild. The last time he had felt this satisfied was when he discovered that his homemade wings worked. The wonder of seeing the brachiosaurus almost made him forget how much trouble they were in.

The Leprechauns were much less impressed, acting as if seeing dinosaurs happened every day. "All right, this is ridiculous. I've got gold to collect and an empire to run," Michael O'Leary declared. "I need out of here and now! NOW! NOW! NOW!" He continued shouting, becoming more and more worked up, seemingly on the verge of hysteria, until Molly punched him in the side of the head. Down he went like a wet towel. Newton wasn't sure if he was just unconscious or dead.

"Honestly!" Molly spat disgustingly, "Some days you'd never guess he was the ruler of the richest empire in the history of empires." She turned her attention to Newton. "If I didn't need you, you'd be dead already. Tell me you have a plan to get us out of here."

The look on Newton's face told her everything she needed to know. There was no plan. "Well, start thinking of one!" she threatened. "Or I start pulling fingernails out!"

Long shadows were falling in the forest and dusk would soon be upon them. Far off, Newton could hear roars from what he could only presume were ferocious, hungry dinosaurs. "If I can make a suggestion," he volunteered, "I think we should move to somewhere more concealed. Out here we're easy targets. At night we won't be able to see any attacks coming."

"You're finally starting to think like a soldier, Pokey," Commander Joe commended him.

"Okay, let's move, then," Molly agreed. "We'll find shelter in the jungle, and first thing in the morning, you better have a plan to get the machine back." She started walking toward the trees.

"What about us?" Herbert asked. "Any chance of undoing these ropes?"

"Nope," Molly replied with an air of finality.

Herbert and Gertrude painfully got up and limped after her without further protest—maybe fearing she'd sock them again. As for Michael O'Leary, he was still splayed out on the ground, unmoving, apparently left to fend for himself. If his guts were plucked out by a pterodactyl or his skull bashed in by a stegosaurus, would Molly even shed a tear? Could someone really be that ruthless?

As they moved toward the forest, Newton mentally burned the location of the pterodactyl nest onto his brain. Molly was walking fast, and Newton had a hard time keeping up with her. When Newton looked over at Max, his best friend shrugged casually, as if to say, "Don't worry, this isn't as bad as it seems." First a wink, now a shrug. Max was certainly putting on a brave face. Not for a second did Newton believe that Max was so upbeat; nonetheless, he appreciated his friend's positivity. It helped him feel slightly less desperate that things would end up horribly. So he shrugged back.

Instead of looking for a path, Molly beelined straight into the jungle, furiously hacking away at vines, doing her best to create some sort of trail through the thick foliage. Compared to the clearing, the jungle was considerably more humid, and soon Newton's shirt was soaked with sweat and he was worried about the unidentifiable creepy-crawlies that occasionally found their way onto him. That these insects had evidently met with the same evolutionary fate as their dinosaur counterparts didn't make them any less worrisome. A red welt that swelled to the size of a baseball appeared on Newton's arm where one particularly hideous grey bug drilled into him before he could squash it into a mess of pungent goop.

As he was pondering the health risks of the bite, Molly stopped abruptly. She sniffed the air. Her eyes narrowed and a look of concentration crossed her face, then she let out a slow smile. "Gold," she announced. "And lots of it, by the aroma wafting up from the ground. Some good may come out of this yet."

She went over and untied Herbert and Gertrude's ropes. The giants were covered in scratches from where the vines had lashed against their skin. Both looked hot and haggard. "Okay, start digging!" Molly ordered.

"Right here?" Herbert asked. "With what?"

"Your hands. Idiot. Now!"

"No one calls my Herbert an idiot!" Gertrude protested, and again made the mistake of lunging at Molly. Before you could say "luck of the Irish!" the Leprechaun punched Gertrude in the other leg, and again the giant crumpled to the ground.

"I said dig!" Molly demanded. "All of you!"

The dirt bit into Newton's nails as he scratched away at the hard ground. His head was dizzy from the heat and yet he didn't dare complain. By the time dark had fallen, the group had made a deep hole in the ground. Newton wondered if Molly, who sat smoking a pipe, glowering over them, was going to make them keep digging all night. He also wondered if Michael was dead or alive, as he still had not returned.

Hours later, exhausted, Newton's brain could barely process that he had hit a solid wall of something. Herbert, Gertrude, Max and Commander Joe also had arrived at the same realization. Instead of digging deeper, they concentrated on scooping away the remaining dirt to reveal a smooth, shiny surface that gleamed in the moonlight.

Molly set her pipe down. "Step away from the hole," she ordered. The group did as instructed, relieved to take a rest from digging. The Leprechaun eased herself into the hole and slowly sank down to her knees. As she put her hands against the cool surface, a look of almost complete bliss overcame her and a line of drool escaped from her mouth. Her eyes crossed and became unfocused. "Gold," she cooed softly, "a vein so pure and so deep that it will change the course of history." Her lips quivered and a tear stole down her cheek. "It's magnificent," she said, before lying down on the smooth surface and seemingly falling into a deep trance.

Seconds, then minutes passed and still Molly lay against the stone. Her breathing grew deeper and deeper, and Newton wondered if she had fallen asleep.

"What should we do?" Max whispered to Newton, as they peered down.

Newton put his finger to his lips, indicating that not another word should be uttered. Using hand signals, he motioned to them to head back in the direction they had hacked their way from. With each step backward, Newton was certain that Molly would wake up and fly into a fury. However, the gold seemed to irresistibly attract her, much the way a magnet does iron.

When they arrived at the edge of the clearing, Newton motioned for everyone to stop. A full moon illuminated the opening. There was no sign of Michael. He had disappeared. "Do you think he's been eaten?" Max asked.

"Let's hope so," Gertrude replied. "One less Leprechaun to deal with would make my toenails sing."

"Keep moving, Pokey," Commander Joe ordered. "We're an easy meal out here. Besides, who knows how long before Molly snaps out of it?"

Herbert wanted to know exactly where they were going.

"To get my time machine back," Newton replied. Stealthily they inched along the edge of the clearing, closing in on the tree where the pterodactyl had deposited the machine. Hopefully the prehistoric bird hadn't decided to move it to a different location while they were digging the hole.

The jungle was eerily silent, a fact that normally would have calmed Newton, but instead made him increasingly nervous. He was certain their group was being watched, but by whom? Or what? At the base of the tree they stopped and looked up, but the nest was lost among the leaves and branches.

"Are you sure this is the right tree?" Commander Joe asked.

"Let's find out!" Gertrude said.

Resting her back against the trunk of the giant arboreal

specimen she started humming a song so out of tune that Newton would not have been surprised to see leaves wilt. Though it made no sense, Newton could swear that the awful noise was causing the bark to vibrate. Gertrude stopped.

"Put the palm of your hand against the tree, Herbie," she instructed.

Herbert followed his wife's wish and soon they were both humming. After about fifteen seconds they stopped. "Are you feeling what I'm feeling?" she asked.

"It's incredible," Herbert whispered.

"Why were you humming? What's so incredible?" Newton asked the giants.

"Were you speaking to the trees?" Max asked.

"Yeah. Sort of," Herbert explained. "The vibration from the humming causes the bark to move, and though it's not exactly talking—it's more a feeling—trees can let you know any number of things."

"Like, this old girl has been around for over three thousand years," Gertrude said. "And I thought the trees in our kingdom had done some living! They've got nothing on her! Also, your machine's definitely up there."

"Then let's move. All this tree-whispering is really touching," Joe said, "but I strongly suggest we get climbing before a roving band of dinosaurs wanders by looking for a late-night snack."

"Good point," Newton agreed. "Let's get vertical."

CHAPTER 11

Because the bark was lined with deep grooves—providing excellent handholds and footholds—and because tree-climbing was one of his all-time favourite hobbies (next to inventing, of course), Newton was looking forward to the climb. Besides, his skills as a tree-climber had increased dramatically after Herbert taught him all of the Merriwart secrets, a considerable repertoire of arboreal ascent techniques.

Newton had barely begun his ascent when he noticed that Max was still rooted to the ground. He hadn't moved. "Wait a second, Gertrude and Herbert," Newton said. "Something's wrong with Max."

Returning to the ground, Newton looked at Max. "You coming or what?"

Max seemed nervous. "I was figuring that maybe I'll just wait here. You know, guard the tree until you guys bring the machine back down." His earlier confidence apparently had vanished.

"Max, there's no way to get the machine down. We have to activate the time-travel sequence up in the nest if we have any hope of escaping. Come on."

A look of pain spread across Max's face. "I can't do it. Just thinking about climbing that high makes my head spin. There's no way I won't slip and plunge to my death."

Commander Joe poked his head out of Newton's shirt pocket. "Well, you're going to end up as a caveman if you stay here. Come on, Max, you've shown more bravery on this trip than I ever thought possible. Pull your big-boy underwear up and let's go."

Max shook his head. "It's no good trying to convince me. Some people can't eat peanut butter, some people can't play a musical instrument, and some people, like me, can't climb more than a couple of feet off the ground without getting dizzy."

"What about my tree fort in the Kingdom of the Merriwarts? You're fine up there."

"That's because the portal takes us directly into your lab. It's not heights, but the climbing part that doesn't agree with me. I'm sorry. I thought you knew that, Newton." It was hard to believe that after all their years together, Newton had failed to realize that his best friend was gripped by this phobia. What could they do? The terrified look on Max's face convinced Newton that he wasn't going to climb, no matter the consequences.

Newton's brain moved at warp speed trying to think of alternative solutions. Commander Joe tapped him on the chest and whispered, "I need to strategize with you in private for a moment, Pokey. Yell to Herbert and Gertrude to get down here ASAP. I might have an idea."

The mini-conference between the giants and Newton lasted only a few moments before Herbert hissed, "You really think I stink that bad?"

Newton and Joe nodded in agreement, while Gertrude cooed, "Nonsense! My man's armpits are the sweetest bouquet this girl has ever inhaled."

Newton didn't have time to argue, but just asked that they give Joe's plan a try. The giants doubtfully agreed.

As they walked over to Max, he eyed them nervously. "I believe we have a solution to your climbing problem," Newton offered. "Do you trust me?"

"Do I have a choice?" Max replied.

"Not really," Newton admitted.

Max sighed dramatically. "Then do what you need to do."

Herbert grabbed Max and cradled his head deep in his armpit. As Commander Joe predicted, it took only a few seconds of inhaling Herbert's pungent body odour before Max was unconscious, knocked out by a smell so foul that a skunk would have turned up his nose in disgust.

Gertrude was shocked, but tried to hide her surprise. "Clearly the human olfactory system isn't nearly as sophisticated as ours."

"Okay, big fellow, take him out of the headlock," Commander Joe ordered. "You don't want to do permanent brain damage. Time to move this operation up and away."

Herbert had no problem climbing and carrying Max under his arm. When Max occasionally let out a groan, threatening to wake up, Herbert administered another whiff of his armpit, and Max would slip back into unconsciousness.

The climb took about half an hour, and by that time the morning light was creeping back into the sky. Because the night was so brief, Newton concluded they must be almost all the way to the North or South Pole. As the group reached the underside of the nest, Newton couldn't believe the size of the thing. It was bigger than a helicopter landing pad. If the pterodactyl was actually in the nest (a very good chance), or a light sleeper (who knew the nocturnal habits of flying dinosaurs?), or organizing a pterodactyl posse (not a pleasant thought) and/or in the mood for a midnight snack (after all, they had already attacked once), Newton knew that this adventure would soon be over.

"Let me go first," Newton offered. "I'll scout the situation."

"Nonsense," Gertrude responded. "We're going to need your brain to get the time machine started." Gertrude then executed some of the most amazing technical climbing moves Newton had ever seen as she navigated the underside of the nest.

Herbert watched in admiration. "I'm the luckiest Merriwart alive. Look at my girl go!"

Newton was surprised that in spite of their extremely dire circumstances, Herbert was feeling so blessed. Love had made him an optimist.

Or a fool.

As Gertrude disappeared over the lip of the nest, Newton braced himself for a horrible round of cawing from an irate pterodactyl, which would invariably be followed by Gertrude's death wails as she unsuccessfully fought the bird.

However, the forest remained silent, and a few moments later, Gertrude reappeared, holding out her hand. "All clear. No sign of anyone."

"And the machine . . . ?" Newton asked.

"Not a trace of it," Gertrude said sombrely. "It's gone."

Gone! Newton felt sick. How could the machine be gone? Where did it go? Newton cursed himself for being so adventurous. He also cursed his curiosity. Why was it necessary for him to see an actual dinosaur? Why couldn't he be like normal people—watch a couple of movies, look at some bones and read books to satisfy this obsession. Instead, now he was cursed to spend the rest of his life in some crappy cave, running away from creatures bigger than cruise ships.

Gertrude smiled. "Just kidding. Your machine's there all right, without a scratch on it. You should have seen the look on your face, Newton!"

Herbert chimed in, "I thought you were going to cry, Newton! It was totally obvious that she was kidding."

Commander Joe just shook his head. "We're in extremely dire circumstances here, people. Lives are on the line. Let's keep the jokes to a minimum."

"Oh lighten up, little man," Gertrude scoffed. "I'm just trying to relax everyone."

Herbert passed Max to Gertrude and she hauled his limp body into the nest. Soon the whole group had climbed inside the massive space. Beside the machine were four eggs, each about the size of a watermelon. Newton put his hand on a fifth, which was slightly smaller. "It's warm," he said.

"I love raw eggs. Anyone in the mood for a little energy boost?" Herbert asked, picking one up.

"Put it down," Commander Joe ordered. "We'll eat later."

"Easy for you to say," Herbert grumbled. "But not all of us have plastic stomachs."

"Put it down. NOW!"

Herbert, sensing that the official Military Consultant might seriously freak out if his orders weren't obeyed, wisely decided to do as instructed.

Max stretched and opened his eyes. "Time for school, Mom?" he asked, obviously still out of it.

"Yes, dear," Gertrude replied. "Actually, you have a big geography test today."

It took a few more minutes of confusion before Max fully woke up. Newton apologized for knocking him out.

"You had no choice," Max assured him.

Suddenly a fierce caw pierced the forest night, and Newton looked up to see a black mass of pterodactyl bearing down on them like a torpedo. Newton ducked, bracing himself for a life-ending blow.

It never came. Herbert, in a rare feat of mental dexterity and Herculean strength, lifted the time machine and held it before them like a shield. The bird hadn't anticipated the move and slammed into the invention. The force of the blow caused Herbert to fall backward, crushing one of the eggs, the machine pinning him down. As for the pterodactyl, it let out an anguished cry as it crashed through the branches, then landed with a heavy thud on the ground.

The silence was broken by Herbert's muffled groan. "Could somebody get this thing off of me!"

Gertrude rushed to his aid. As Herbert stood up, Newton saw that his butt was covered in broken egg. Instantly a swarm of bees were at him, a hungry mass of creatures intent on a free lunch. It took only a few moments for them to ingest every last trace of egg. They were gone as quickly as they came.

"That's what I call a feeding frenzy!" Herbert said.

Newton couldn't believe they had once again avoided death.

"Excellent work, soldier," Commander Joe told Herbert. "Learn a little personal hygiene and, who knows, you might be military material after all."

"Oh, Herbie," Gertrude swooned. "You're a hero! Let me make sure your toes aren't bruised." And to everyone's disgust, Herbert lifted a leg and Gertrude started slurping.

"I'm going to be sick," Max said, and indeed he did look green enough to lose his lunch.

Newton quickly realized that he had bigger concerns to deal with. Though he was extremely grateful to be alive, the feeling soon dissolved and was replaced with dread as he looked at his machine. There was a huge dent where the bird crashed into it. Wires poked out from places they shouldn't have .

Commander Joe obviously shared his concern. "Tell me it looks worse than it actually is."

"Or then again, it might be *worse* than it actually *looks*," Newton replied.

"You serious?"

"Possibly. I'm not sure," Newton said honesty. The sky had brightened enough to assess the damage. The group remained silent as the inventor poked at the machine, hoping against hope that nothing was irreparably broken. Incredibly, even the fickle atomic warper appeared mostly intact. "I think I just might be able to fix this," Newton replied. "Max, do you still have your magnifying glass?"

Max reached into the front pocket of his shirt and pulled out one scientific-strength magnifying glass. "And to think I thought this might be unnecessary," he said proudly.

"Obviously you were wrong." Newton positioned the lens in such a way that the heat from a sunbeam could solder the broken wires together. Meanwhile, the rest of the group kept watch on the sky, expecting the return of more pterodactyls. Below, a pair of brachiosaurus were ripping apart the dead bird. Newton would have found it fascinating, except that he had more pressing matters to deal with.

"So? What do you think? Are we getting out of here?" Max asked worriedly, when Newton finally stepped away from the machine.

"Well, there's only one way to find out," Newton replied, and started programming the machine. Given the damage it had sustained, he felt the odds were slim that it would work.

Before he had a chance to find out, his actions were interrupted by an unexpected arrival.

"You weren't planning on leaving without us, now were you?" Molly asked menacingly.

Newton turned and saw that the Leprechaun was standing on the edge of the nest. Michael, very much alive, was beside her. They weren't smiling.

"How'd you get up here?" Gertrude asked. "We didn't hear you."

"The oaf didn't hear us? What a surprise," Michael O'Leary mocked. "As the world's greatest thieves, masters of stealth, if we were in the mood, we could steal the hair from your head without being detected. Of course you didn't hear us!"

Molly walked over to Newton and grabbed him by the ear. Pain radiated to the tips of his toes and he wondered if she was going to rip the earlobe right off. He could smell the mint on the little fiend's breath.

"Let's make one thing rainbow clear," Molly hissed. "Any more funny stuff and you'll wish you were dead. Get us back to our kingdom NOW!"

She let go of Newton's ear. His head rang with pain.

Newton was angry. Probably because they were already in so much danger, Molly didn't have nearly the terrifying effect on him that she might have. He was not a boy who enjoyed having his earlobes viciously tugged. EVER! Still, he knew better than to mess with Michael or Molly.

"Okay," he said, "everybody huddle in closely and I'll start the machine."

"No. I don't think so," Michael said. "The giants and the funny-looking kid, they stay. You, nerd, you're coming with us." He pointed at Newton.

Newton had always known that he wasn't the coolest kid around, but he definitely wasn't a *nerd*! That comment hurt more than the twisted earlobe. *How dare they call me a nerd!* He knew arguing with the Leprechauns was useless and trying to overpower them was worse than foolhardy. There had to be another solution.

But what?

His attention rested on the pterodactyl eggs.

He turned to his friends. "I'm sorry, guys. There's nothing I can do. The machine probably won't work anyway."

"Don't feel bad, Newton," Max said. "If I were you, I'd do the same thing."

"At least we have each other," Herbert said, smiling at Gertrude.

"If you ever get back to our kingdom," Gertrude said in a brave voice, "you'll make sure to tell them what happened to us."

Newton nodded. "I will," he replied as sadly as he could, hoping Molly and Michael would buy his performance.

"These goodbyes are breaking my heart, but let's get moving," Michael O'Leary demanded.

Newton put his hand on his chin and examined the time machine. "Something's wrong," he announced.

Molly eyed him suspiciously. "You're stalling. Put the machine into gear!"

Newton took a deep breath. The success of his plan depended on the next few moments. "Okay. But something's not right and I can't figure out what." He set the countdown clock for T minus thirty seconds.

At T minus twenty seconds, he shouted, "Wait, I know what it is! The rod that stabilizes the velocity booster is missing!" Frantically he punched at the control panel, but the machine kept counting down. "It's not stopping. Quick! Everyone search the nest. There still might be time to find it!"

The countdown read T minus ten seconds.

Pretending to search for the missing rod, Newton rushed over to the pterodactyl eggs, picked two of them up and hurled them at Molly and Michael. His marksmanship (for once in his life) was perfect. The eggs bull's-eyed the Leprechauns, covering their faces in gunk. A swarm of bees instantly materialized and blinded Molly and Michael. They staggered around, swatting at their faces, desperately trying to get the bees off.

T minus three seconds and Newton shouted, "QUICK, EVERYONE! INTO THE MACHINE!"

Closing his eyes, Newton dove, hoping against hope that he hadn't mistimed the move. He prayed that Molly and Michael were blinded by the bees and wouldn't be able to react quickly enough. He also prayed that the time machine still worked—he hated to contemplate what Michael and Molly would do to him if it didn't.

Unfortunately he was the first one to dive into the transporter. If you've ever had the bad luck of being on the bottom of a pileup that includes two giants, you might have some idea of the pain Newton experienced.

When he opened his eyes a moment later, Newton felt like his entire body had been fed through a paper shredder.

"Get off of me!" Newton grunted. "I can't breathe." Newton had had the wind knocked out of him, but the pain he was experiencing made him realize he was very much alive. All he could see was a pterodactyl egg beside him. He had failed. They hadn't gone anywhere.

However, when he lifted his head he realized that he was wrong. They were now in a green field, scattered around the time machine. If Newton had had the breath to do so, he would have shouted for joy.

After a few moments he sat up. Herbert and Gertrude appeared as stunned as he felt. "Where's Max?"

Commander Joe lifted his head out of the flap of Newton's shirt and looked around. "I'm sure he made it, Pokey."

But his friend was nowhere in sight. Newton stood, now getting frantic.

How could he have abandoned Max? The relief that Molly and Michael had been left 140 million years in the dust was replaced by the worst feeling Newton had ever experienced. His best friend was alone, left to face the wrath of two evil Leprechauns. Though he tried to rationalize that there was nothing he could have done about it, Newton was devastated. After all, this adventure was entirely his idea.

He imagined the look on Max's mother's face when she learned what had happened to her son. "We have to go back!" Newton declared. "I can't leave Max there."

"What happens if we're too late?" Herbert asked.

"That's a chance we'll have to take," Commander Joe said. "We don't leave soldiers behind. Ever. It's part of the code."

As Newton began reprogramming the time machine, a muffled cough came from near Herbert.

"Hey, there's a critter underneath me!" Herbert exclaimed. He stood up and, much to everyone's astonishment, there was Max, dazed but very much alive.

"Arghh!" Max said spitting. "When I dove, I landed right in Herbert's butt. It knocked me out again!"

Never had Newton felt so deliriously happy. *My best friend is alive! Molly and Michael are gone!* Newton jumped up and down chanting, "We made it! We made it!"

Unfortunately his happiness was short-lived. For one thing, his time machine started smoking and before anyone had a chance to react, it was engulfed in flames.

But Newton didn't have much of a chance to contemplate the destruction of his beloved invention or even get upset, because a far graver situation presented itself.

An angry mob of Leprechauns marched toward them, brandishing rifles. Newton picked up the pterodactyl egg, put it in his knapsack and watched as they came closer, wondering if they would shoot first and ask questions later.

CHAPTER 12

"What have you done with Michael and Molly?" an ancient, crusty Leprechaun demanded.

Newton scanned the green faces, looking for a friendly Leprechaun among the bunch. Unfortunately there wasn't one. This brigade was about as welcoming as the last group they had encountered, when Simon snuck them in through the vaults.

As Newton contemplated what to say, he was overcome with a monstrous exhaustion. He yawned, more tired than scared. "They're gone," he said matter-of-factly. "And they're not coming back."

The ancient Leprechaun roughly poked the end of his rifle into Newton's gut. "You're lying. There's no way you defeated them. Molly and Michael are fierce warriors."

"Who made a tactical mistake," countered Max, "by underestimating Newton's genius."

It took Newton and his friends a few minutes to explain

what had happened. Newton considered inventing some fabulous story where it wasn't their fault that Molly and Michael ended up being left behind, but in the end he was just too tired to go to the effort. The way he figured it, most likely they were going to be hanged anyway, so what good would lying do?

When their story was finished, a look of surprise was etched on the ancient Leprechaun's face. In fact, the entire group looked shocked. "So you mean to tell me our leaders are stuck 140 million years back in time? Is there any chance of them ever returning?"

"The only way is if I go and get them," said Newton. "And it's not happening without a time machine." He pointed to his smoking invention. Even the most technically challenged individual would admit that the machine was burned beyond hope. "Besides, I've seen all the live dinosaurs I need to in this life."

"I kind of liked it there," Gertrude said.

"Me too," agreed Herbert.

Newton chose to ignore the giants' endorsements of prehistoric tourism. "Absolutely no way," he said with finality. He would have added, Not even if you tortured me, but was worried the Leprechauns might see that as an appealing challenge.

The ancient Leprechaun sighed deeply and looked nervously to his comrades. For some reason Newton's information had the effect of turning them into a shy bunch. They stared at the ground, no longer daring to make eye contact with him. Newton could have sworn that the ancient guy seemed nervous.

"Follow me," said the Leprechaun, this time not nearly so aggressively. In fact, he was rather polite about the request.

Once again they were marched down the main street and once again Leprechauns stopped whatever they were doing to stare at the foreigners.

"What do you think, Newton?" Max asked. "Are they going to kill us?"

"No. I don't think so," Newton replied, but perhaps he was just too tired to think rationally. They walked past the main square and Newton was relieved to see that no one was about to be hanged. At the entrance to Molly and Michael's castle, the Leprechauns ushered Newton and his group in first.

"What's going on, Pokey?" Commander Joe asked. "What's your gut tell you?"

"My gut tells me that I haven't eaten in a while," Newton whispered back.

They stopped before the golden thrones of Molly and Michael. "Take a seat . . . please," the ancient Leprechaun said, though the effort to be polite looked like it cost him considerable energy.

"Who?" Newton asked.

"Just you," the Leprechaun said. "You're in charge now."

You're in charge now! Newton thought he must be delirious. "What did you say?" he asked.

"You're in charge. It will all be explained. Please, take a seat."

Because the Leprechauns were small, the throne was child-sized. Newton had no problem fitting in, but the proportions made the seat seem significantly less regal than he'd have liked.

"How about me? Can I take the other seat?" Max asked.

"No. Just the inventor. He's the chosen one."

Of all the strange things that Newton had ever seen or heard, this had to be the weirdest. *The chosen one?* What were they talking about?

Within moments, the doors to the great room opened and in marched more Leprechauns, weighed down with huge trays of food—roasted pig surrounded by potatoes and carrots and smothered in gravy. Salads piled high with ripe tomatoes. Fruit platters with pieces cut into intricate designs. The last tray held a six-tiered cake with white frosting that wouldn't look out of place at a royal wedding. Newton's stomach started doing backflips just thinking about eating. Herbert was drooling like a dog looking for scraps at the dinner table. Gertrude was practically panting.

Max hissed, "I wonder if the food is poisoned?"

"Well, if this is our last meal, I can think of worse ways to die," Gertrude replied.

To be honest, Newton felt the same way—though he seriously doubted that their hosts would have gone to all this effort just to poison him. Why wouldn't they simply have shot them? Not bothering with utensils, Newton started shoving food into his mouth. It was ugly, but his friends (with the exception of Commander Joe, who never needed to eat) were equally ill-mannered. Now that the danger of the adventure had been downgraded from red alert, Newton couldn't remember ever being hungrier. The food was fantastic. Even the salad. Leprechauns might not be the friendliest creatures but they sure knew how to cook a feast. With Herbert and Gertrude responsible for the bulk of the consuming, all the food eventually disappeared.

Commander Joe shook his head at the eating spectacle before him. "I've seen apes with better table manners. That was disgusting!"

"Delicious with a capital BURP!" said Herbert satisfactorily, and he let out a belch so foul that the Leprechauns stepped back for safety, most likely afraid that their ears would lose their pointiness. Gertrude breathed in the gas deeply, like she was smelling the world's most aromatic bouquet.

For his part, Newton was too tired to care if he'd made a pig of himself eating the pig. His eyelids were being pulled down by extreme gravity. There was nothing he could do to keep them open and he felt himself sliding off the throne, dreaming of parachuting.

"Get Newton to bed!" ordered the ancient Leprechaun.

Eight pairs of strong hands picked him up and whisked Newton to the royal chamber. Of course the bed was much too short and his feet stuck out of the end. To rectify the problem, Molly's bed was shoved over so that Newton had more than enough room.

"What about us? Where are we sleeping?" Max asked.

Newton threw him a pillow. "Here—the carpet looks pretty soft." And it did. Newton would have been glad to sleep on the carpet. He would have been glad to sleep on a dirt floor. He would have been glad to sleep just about anywhere at that point. Max must have felt the same way, because he took the pillow without further protest and flopped down on the floor.

When Newton woke up (four hours and thirty-six minutes later, according to Commander Joe), his plastic pal was on the pillow beside him.

"What's that noise?" Newton asked. "Somebody working a chainsaw?" Indeed it sounded as if a tree was being cut down right in the room.

"Yep. Herbert and Gertrude have been sawing logs for hours," Commander Joe said. "I'm surprised they didn't wake you up."

Newton turned and saw Herbert and Gertrude cuddled together, face to face. Max too was still sound asleep, his thumb stuck in his mouth. (When Max eventually woke up, Newton pretended he hadn't noticed.)

Newton got out of the bed feeling better than he had in a long time, marvelling at the restorative powers of a few hours' sleep. By his calculations, they had been gone fifty-two hours. Newton had barely finished stretching his arms when two important-looking Leprechauns marched in. Newton could tell they were important because they had long beards and wore glasses and intricate gold necklaces. The fact that three dozen Leprechauns marched solemnly behind them was also an indication of their status.

"Top of the afternoon to you. Are you ready for your coronation today, King Newton?"

King? They couldn't possibly be talking to him—could they? Surely there was a Leprechaun also named Newton, standing directly behind him that he had failed to notice.

He turned and looked.

There wasn't.

"Did you say, 'King'?" Newton gulped as he turned back to the Leprechauns.

One of the important Leprechauns snapped his fingers, and another, obviously less-important Leprechaun scurried forward, carrying an ancient book. He bowed respectfully, before opening the volume.

The important Leprechaun cleared his throat. "Allow me to introduce myself. I am Seamus O'Neill, Chief Officiating Officer of the Royal Leprechaun Monarchy Association." Seamus bowed to Newton, then cleared his throat dramatically before reading:

> According to the laws of succession for the ancient Tribe of Leprechauns, there are three conditions required for a new King or Queen to be crowned.
>
> 1. The closest blood relative of the reigning King or Queen shall in turn become King or Queen.
> 2. In the event that there are no blood relatives, the person who had the last confirmed contact with either the King or Queen becomes the heir.

3. That person must have in his or her posses-
    sion the Royal Four-Leaf Clover.

Seamus stopped reading. "And that's you, Newton."

"Impossible," Newton replied.

"Perhaps there was something in the laws of succession that you didn't understand? Let's review, shall we?" Seamus said, sounding an awful lot like Mr. Mesesnel, Newton's former grade-two teacher.

And so began the lesson on how Newton would become King. "Even though Molly and Michael seized the throne by force, the fact that they were recognized as our rulers established a new line of succession. Add to this, they were both only children of only children of only children. As a result, neither had cousins. Add to this that they had no children of their own and it becomes fairly clear: no children, no heirs, no blood relatives. The first condition can't be fulfilled."

Seamus continued. "So we must now turn our attention to the second condition: 'In the event that there are no blood relatives, the person who had the last confirmed contact with either the King or Queen becomes the heir.' You are the last person who had contact with them 140 million years ago. Correct?"

Newton couldn't disagree with his logic up to that point.

"Finally, there is only one Royal Four-Leaf Clover, and you have it."

"I'm sorry to tell you, but that's where you made a terrible mistake," he informed them. Newton knew for a fact that he didn't have the clover. The night the Leprechauns were chasing him and Witch Hazel, Newton ditched the clover.

Seamus smiled sagely. "Reach into your left pocket."

Uncertainly, Newton fished around and pulled out the contents: some loose change, his pocket knife, a folded-up piece of paper that contained his initial thoughts on an invention so secret Newton hadn't even named it yet, and a compass.

"Nope, there's no four-leaf clover here," he declared.

"Open the piece of paper," Seamus instructed.

Newton carefully unfolded the paper, keeping it close to his chest in case any aspiring inventors wanted to steal a glance. Stuck in a crease was the Royal Four-Leaf Clover. How had it ended up in there?

"Don't forget we are the world's greatest thieves. We can putpocket just as easily as we can pickpocket. The night with Witch Hazel, your instincts were correct. There was a tracking device in the clover. When we discovered you wandering in Macgillycuddy's Reeks, Michael and Molly insisted that we get the clover back to you in case something unexpected happened. After you 'mysteriously' passed out, we slipped the clover back in."

"But what if I had changed my pants?"

Seamus gave him a droll look. "Considering your personal hygiene, the odds of that were very, very low. Besides, we figured that that piece of paper was most likely extremely valuable to you."

"How?"

The Leprechaun smiled smugly. "You don't really want me to tell everyone what your next big invention might be, do you?"

Newton absolutely didn't, so the contents of the piece of

paper were not discussed any further. Newton examined the clover but could not figure out how a tracking device could be inserted into a piece of metal thin enough to be hidden in a clover leaf. It was an engineering marvel that the inventing part of his brain would have enjoyed pondering more, but for now that conundrum would have to be put on hold.

He had kingly concerns to deal with.

Newton debated continuing to argue that there was no way he should be the Leprechauns' supreme ruler, but then he reasoned that being King was probably much, much better than not being King. Especially among these folks.

"Okay, I believe you. I'm King. So what's next?"

"Whatever you want," Seamus replied. "I have no authority to tell our King what to do. Actually, it works the other way around. You're usually the one giving orders."

Newton liked the sound of that.

"Order some more of that cake," Max whispered. "Herbert and Gertrude pigged out on it before I got so much as a lick."

"Well . . . ," Newton began, and rubbed his hand under his chin because he thought that looked extremely regal. "I order everyone to leave this chamber at once. Everyone except Herbert, Gertrude, Max and Commander Joe, that is. I need some time to think. To decide what changes are in order in this kingdom. Please." He added "please" because he didn't want everyone thinking he was one of those mean kings.

Seamus bowed deeply. "As you wish, Your Highness."

* * *

When the Leprechauns had cleared out, Commander Joe jumped around excitedly. "Do you know what this means, Pokey? It means that we're stinking filthy rich!"

Newton hadn't really thought of the consequences of having control of the world's biggest gold reserve. "I suppose we are," he said. "But we've got more important matters to deal with right now."

"What could be more important than unlimited wealth?" Max demanded.

His life no longer in immediate danger, Newton now remembered that there were higher priorities than money. "Well, a few things," he replied. "We need to figure out what happened to Witch Hazel and why her house burned down. We need to get Lester out of jail and also hope that Prince Raphael hasn't taken over the Merriwart kingdom by now. Not to mention, we promised Simon that we'd come back for him."

"What are you talking about, Newton?" Gertrude asked. "My brother is back in the kingdom? Lester's in jail?"

Newton realized he had never filled Gertrude in on all that had happened since she was kidnapped. "Yeah. He showed up right after you went missing."

Gertrude paused. "I smell something rotten."

"Maybe it's your toes," Commander Joe offered.

Gertrude ignored the comment, while Herbert lifted her foot and took a whiff. "What are the chances that my deadbeat brother, who hasn't seen the Merriwart sun in over a century, shows up as soon as I'm gone?"

"Are you suggesting that he was in on the Leprechauns' plan?" Max asked. "That he was working for the enemy?"

"I wouldn't put anything beneath him."

"Let's try to piece this together," Newton suggested, trying to get the Sherlock Holmes part of his brain working. "How are all these events related?"

"You mean Prince Raphael's appearance, and Witch Hazel's disappearance and/or possible murder?" Commander Joe asked.

"That's exactly what I mean."

"Well, there is one way to find out," Max volunteered.

"How?" Newton was surprised to find that Max just might have out-thought him.

"You could use your kingly powers and order the Leprechauns to tell you."

This was such an excellent idea that Newton wished he had invented it himself.

CHAPTER 13

By the time Seamus finished explaining just how everything had fit together in the Leprechauns' scheme to amass the world's entire gold supply, Newton's jaw was almost on the ground—he was that flabbergasted. Leprechauns were far more dastardly than he had imagined. And Newton had already seen enough dastardly behaviour from these little people to have formed a low opinion of them.

The long and (definitely) short of it was that the Leprechauns hadn't left anything to chance. Prince Raphael and Witch Hazel were simply an insurance policy.

Their plan worked like this. The Leprechauns knew that the Merriwarts didn't have a leader, because, of course, they had kidnapped her. They also knew that if the kingdom was in chaos, the giants would never come after the Leprechauns— even in the unlikely event that their crime was detected. They brought Raphael in to create this chaos, and thus avoid dealing with a mob of Merriwarts on their doorstep.

"We found Prince Raphael and convinced him that a huge injustice had been done: the Merriwart throne was up for grabs and he should have been King."

A look of enlightenment crossed Gertrude's face. "Of course. It makes perfect sense. If Raphael thought the crown was his, he would claim it, no matter if the rest of the kingdom disagreed."

"And his excesses know no limits—even by Merriwart standards," Herbert added.

If that were the case Newton knew this struggle for power might get ugly, for the Merriwarts weren't a race known for backing down from an argument with their own.

"What about Witch Hazel?" he asked.

Seamus looked uncomfortable before—now he was a fidgeting mess. Twice he opened his mouth to explain, twice he shut it.

Newton gulped. The Leprechaun's silence confirmed his worst fears. "She's dead, isn't she?" he croaked.

Seamus looked uncomfortable.

Witch Hazel dead? Newton blinked, once, twice, and then the tears started flowing. He was overcome with a sadness that felt like lead. There was no way she was dead—and yet . . .

"But why?" Newton asked. "What threat could she possibly be?"

"With the Merriwart kingdom in shambles, Hazel was your only link to other worlds, to places where we might not be able to find you quite as easily should we need your services. We couldn't take the risk that you might disappear," Seamus explained. "The order was given to burn her house down."

Newton felt something harden inside him. His eyes narrowed. "I want to see the entire kingdom out in the courtyard in an hour."

"Everyone?" Seamus asked in surprise.

"Even the babies! Now, RUN!" Newton ordered, trying to suppress a rage that was welling up inside him.

"You all right, Pokey?" Commander Joe asked as soon as the Leprechauns had left. "You're not planning on doing anything you're going to regret. Are you?"

"I'm not sure," Newton replied.

And indeed he wasn't. After all, they had killed Witch Hazel.

Flanked by his friends, Newton stared out at the sea of green faces. The entire Leprechaun population numbered 6,354. There was a nervousness in the air. From the moment Seamus had left, Newton had stewed over what he was going to say and what he was going to do. At last an idea had come to him.

"As you are aware," Newton began, speaking into the microphone that had been set up for him, "I am your new leader. As you are also aware, these past ninety-two years under the rule of Michael and Molly have seen Leprechauns transform themselves from a gentle race of people into a gold-hungry mob that will stop at nothing to obtain yet one more flake of the metal. Witches have been murdered, Trolls killed, kingdoms destroyed, countless fortunes stolen—simply to fulfill this lust." Newton paused. "So the question that must be asked is this: how am I going to get rid of all this ill-gained gold?"

Leprechauns turned to one another, looks of disbelief on their faces. *Get rid of their precious gold?* The idea was beyond comprehension.

"Something must be done, but no matter how hard I've tried, I can't figure out an answer. So this is my proposal: I want every member of the kingdom over the age of three to come up with an idea, write it on a piece of paper and put it in the Royal Suggestion Box. Adults will help those who can't write. When I return, I will read the answers." Newton paused and looked solemnly at the assembly before him. "Heaven help you if it turns out no one can think of a suitable suggestion. Seamus will be in charge of collecting your proposals."

"But where are you going?" Seamus asked under his breath.

"Back to the Kingdom of the Merriwarts, to make sure Prince Raphael hasn't destroyed the forest."

Fortunately the Leprechauns had a portal that led directly to the kingdom. Unfortunately, what the friends saw when they got there confirmed their worst fears about Raphael.

"What has he done?" gasped Gertrude.

"What kind of extreme makeover is this?" Herbert asked. Every trunk of every tree in the Merriwart forest had been painted a shade of hot pink so bright that it hurt Newton's eyes. Loud banging could be heard high in the trees. It was coming from the banquet hall. Garbage was strewn everywhere. Tree branches were broken, their limbs lying for-lornly on the ground.

Gertrude scurried up the banquet hall tree faster than Newton had ever thought a giant could move. Herbert followed.

Gasping, Newton, Max, and Commander Joe arrived at the banquet hall a few minutes after Gertrude and Herbert. Though the Merriwarts were not known for their hygienic ways, they had sunk to a new low. Piles of food lay rotting everywhere. Swarms of fruit flies gorged on the bounty. Newton was certain that the movement he saw on the heaps was maggots crawling around, but because he didn't want to barf, he didn't dare go in for a closer look to confirm this theory. In short, it appeared that a party of monstrous proportions had been raging since they left.

In the centre of the banquet hall was Prince Raphael, banging furiously on a set of primitive drums and wailing. If Newton hadn't seen the smile on his face, he would have thought the giant was in extreme agony. Newton covered his ears. About fifty Merriwarts were scattered around the hall, slouching in chairs or lying on the floor, deep in sleep and snoring loudly, in spite of the awful noise.

"SHUT UP!" Gertrude roared from the entranceway.

Immediately Prince Raphael stopped singing and drumming. "Who dares interrupt my concert?" he demanded, looking around furiously. Surprisingly, none of the sleeping Merriwarts woke up.

"I do," Gertrude replied, and walked to the front of the hall. "What have you done to my kingdom?"

Prince Raphael belched and, without even saying "excuse

me," replied, "Call me King. I am the new ruler of the Merriwarts. You left your people. I order you to sit down at once and allow me to finish my performance. I'm just getting to the good part."

Gertrude's eyes turned hard and her face went blotchy with rage. "You're what?" she exploded. "I've been gone only three days! You can't be king! And what happened to our trees?"

"Don't you just love it? Brown bark is so boring. Hot pink says Merriwarts are ready to party."

"Have you had a complete brain freeze?" Gertrude demanded, sounding more impatient by the second.

Raphael smiled smugly. "Get used to the changes, sis. There's a new king in town and he's ready to rock your—"

Gertrude slapped him so hard that Newton wouldn't have been surprised if she knocked a few molars loose.

"Whoa!" Commander Joe whispered.

Newton and Max stepped back, fully expecting an all-out brawl to erupt.

Instead of retaliating, the prince did something even more shocking.

He started to cry. "That really hurt. You've always been a meany," he blubbered.

"And you've always been an idiot! Look at this place. It's appalling!" Gertrude retorted. "More importantly, why don't you tell me all about your good friends the Leprechauns?"

Prince Raphael hung his head. "How'd you know about that?" he asked sheepishly.

"Because those same Leprechauns kidnapped me and Herbert!"

"And you actually got away?" Raphael asked, impressed.

"Just barely," Gertrude spat. "Mom and Dad would be ashamed of your behaviour. This is low, even for you."

Raphael looked humiliated. "I'm sorry. I'm such a bad giant. The Leprechauns told me that you had fallen down a pit and died and that the Merriwarts desperately needed a new leader."

Gertrude shook her head. "I can tell when you're lying."

"Mom always told me I had very regal bearing," he offered lamely.

"*Weasel* bearing. She said you were a weasel."

"Are you sure?"

"Positive."

Raphael turned red. "Well, that does make a bit more sense, now that you mention it."

The destruction that Raphael had wreaked on the kingdom in such a short period was staggering. Merriwarts were passed out everywhere from drinking Herculean quantities of Bliss (the Merriwarts' national drink). Tree forts, including Newton's, had been trashed. Floorboards were missing and holes punched in walls. Clothes hung from tree branches. All because Prince Raphael's first order since assuming the throne was "Live it up at all costs." The Merriwarts loved any excuse for a party, so the ingredients were in place to cook up a gigantic mess.

"What would have happened if I'd been gone longer?" Gertrude demanded.

"Well, I had big plans," Raphael answered sheepishly. "My next decree would have been to start construction on a huge slide that stretched from the banquet hall all the way to the ground. I was going to grease it with Jell-O and then have a Merriwart Slide Olympics. I know—it's a stupid idea."

"I bet I'd be pretty good at that," Herbert mused. "I've always loved sliding."

Gertrude looked from Herbert to Raphael, her interest piqued. "You might be on to something there. Maybe we should discuss this further."

"Really?" Raphael said, looking surprised and slightly less humiliated. "I've got some drawings if you want to take a look—"

"What about Lester?" Newton asked, cutting the conversation short. "In case you've forgotten, we still need to rescue him."

Gertrude cast her gaze at the ground. Herbert wouldn't make eye contact with Newton either, instead focusing on the tip of his finger, which only moments before had been lodged alarmingly far up his nose.

"Well . . . ?" Newton asked impatiently, wondering what the giants were balking at. Lester was their dear friend.

Gertrude looked up guiltily. "Don't take this the wrong way, Newton, but I think it might be better if you handled the Lester situation yourself."

"I don't understand where you're going with this," Newton said. "Are you saying you're not planning to rescue Lester?"

"No. Not at all. But think about it. If Lester got caught by the police, it's almost certain that we'd meet the same fate. We'll go if you want us to—but don't you think we'd do more harm than good?"

"Gertrude makes a valid argument. A couple of giants would stick out like . . . well, giants," Commander Joe said.

"What about brute force?" Max offered. "I mean, maybe their size could work to our advantage."

"In most cases I'd agree, but size is the reason Lester landed himself in so much trouble in the first place," Joe said.

It was agreed that the giants would stay behind while Newton and his crew attempted to get Lester back to his trees.

"Just maybe the slide will be done by then," Herbert added hopefully.

Sometimes Merriwarts had a difficult time prioritizing.

CHAPTER 14

Not bothering to go home (though Max phoned his mother to tell her he was still alive), the group beelined for the portal that led straight to the jail. Newton had never been inside a police station before and was surprised by how intimidating everything seemed.

As they approached the front desk, Commander Joe whispered to Newton, "What's the plan, Pokey?"

Before Newton had a chance to reply, the desk sergeant practically spat out, "Can I help you miscreants?"

"Yes, sir," Newton replied. He added the "sir" part because he had read once that law enforcement officers got a little testy if you didn't give them respect. "Do you happen to have a giant locked up here by the name of Lester?"

The sergeant, whose name tag read Buster, leaned over his desk and glared at Newton. "Who's asking?"

Newton wondered if the sergeant thought there was a ventriloquist in the police station. "I am," Newton replied, trying not to sound like a smart aleck, though this was one of the stupidest questions he'd ever heard.

"That's classified information," the sergeant replied.

"Even for his friends?" Max asked.

The sergeant ignored Max's question and busied himself with paperwork.

"EVEN FOR HIS FRIENDS?" Max repeated, this time more forcefully.

"I don't like your tone, son," Sergeant Buster warned.

"I don't care," Max replied. "I want to see my friend. NOW! Or I start writing down badge numbers."

"Has your best friend lost his mind?" Commander Joe whispered to Newton.

Newton wondered the same thing, especially when he saw Max's smug smile. They both watched as Buster's face turned eight shades of red. It seemed to take all of the sergeant's willpower not to reach over the desk and wallop Max.

"GET OUT OF MY POLICE STATION!" the sergeant bellowed. "You're lucky I don't arrest you for disrespecting the law."

Incredibly, Max didn't move. He didn't even flinch. "Well, first, for your information, the only disrespect that's happening around here is yours for us. And second, as any moron knows, there's no such law."

"Are you calling me a MORON?"

Max breathed in deeply and dramatically, as if trying to keep himself calm. He spoke to the sergeant like a frustrated parent to a very annoying child. "Not yet. But if I don't see my friend in the next two minutes, you're going to wish that was all I had done."

If Newton weren't actually witnessing this exchange, he never would have believed it. This couldn't be happening. And yet, against all odds, it was. Had Max suddenly developed a death wish? Or had he just utterly lost his mind?

"That's it kid, you're under arrest!" Sergeant Buster shouted, bringing out a pair of handcuffs and stepping around his desk. "I hope the judge sends you to juvenile detention until you're a senior citizen."

Still Max held his composure, seemingly unaffected by the threat of jail time. He casually reached into his back pocket and pulled out what looked like a business card. He handed it to Sergeant Buster.

"What's this?" the burly officer asked.

"Read it," Max replied. He waited a couple of beats and added dramatically, "And weep."

When the sergeant read the card, he did look like he might weep. He definitely blinked a couple of tears away. His moustache twitched and his hands trembled. The handcuffs slipped out of his grasp and clanked to the ground.

"Right this way, gentlemen," Sergeant Buster replied. "I am so sorry about the delay. Please accept my deepest apologies." He tried to hand back Max's card, but Max crossed his hands over his chest and refused to accept it.

"Why don't you keep that for now. Maybe forever, depending on how things go."

As they sat in the visitors' room waiting for Lester to be brought in, Newton leaned over to Max and whispered,

"What did I miss? What just happened back there?"

Max smiled. "Have you forgotten what my father does?"

"I have a photographic memory. Besides everyone knows that your dad is the doughnut king of Mulmur." It was true. Don Brown, a.k.a. Doughnut Don, had cornered the market for hundreds of miles. In fact, his cinnamon twists were so popular, people flew in from as far away as Amsterdam to buy them. But nowhere were his doughnuts more popular than at the precincts. To a badge, police officers adored the sugary creations. And Don, a former security guard, adored cops. It didn't hurt that to thank them for keeping the streets safe, Don gave them all the doughnuts they could eat—for free.

Don was aware that occasionally Max had issues with bullies and he worried that things might one day get out of hand, so he gave him a special card—to be used only in extreme emergencies. The card read:

I GIVE MY SON, MAX BROWN, THE POWER TO BAN YOU FROM DON'S DOUGHNUTS FOR LIFE. YOU WILL NEVER BE ALLOWED TO STEP INTO ONE OF MY STORES AGAIN. EVER. NO TAKE-BACKS. GRANNY, GRANNY TWO-SHOES.

Newton couldn't decide what was more amazing: that such a card existed or that Max hadn't used it before. After all, he tended to get picked on even more than Newton.

"Newton! Max!" Lester shouted, when Buster led him in. His hands were handcuffed behind his back and his ankles were shackled.

Simply put, he looked awful—like he'd aged a hundred years in three days. His standard-issue orange prisoner's uniform looked to be two sizes too small for him and there were open sores on his face, neck and hands. His skin was the grey of winter slush.

Newton felt a lump in his throat. The sight of Lester broke his heart.

The giant sat down. "You okay, Lester?" Newton asked.

"No. I can't even pretend to be. I think I'm dying. You've got to get me out of here, Newton. Much longer in this place and I'm terrified my lungs are going to shut down and my heart will stop beating. I need to be in the trees, smelling the leaves."

"What did they charge you with?"

"Well, that's the thing. I sort of had a freak-out," Lester replied. "Well, actually a major meltdown. After they brought me to the station and I realized what jail was, I completely lost it. Went bonkers." Lester looked down at the table in shame.

"What did you do?" Newton asked gently.

"I kind of broke a couple of officers' noses with all my thrashing around. It was a mis—"

"They had to go to the hospital—in an ambulance!" Buster interjected. "This big old oaf could have killed them. As it stands now, he's up on assault charges!"

Max glared at the police officer. "Silence."

Newton swallowed hard. Assault charges! "Is this true?" he whispered to Lester.

"It's true," Lester said so sadly that surely a piece of the giant's heart must have broken.

As he sat on the steps outside the police station, Newton's brain worked furiously to figure out what they could do to get Lester out of prison. Even the threat of Max's card made no difference—no one but a judge had the power to release the giant. Buster told them it would be weeks, possibly months before the case went before a judge. And who knows how long the trial would last. They all agreed that the situation was desperate—immediate action was necessary because Lester wouldn't be able to hang in there much longer.

Newton pressed his hands against the sides of his head, hoping the pressure would squeeze his brain into brilliance. He closed his eyes and the colour green flooded his thoughts. Why green? He never had green thoughts. It must be significant. What began as a colour quickly morphed into a form. As the form took shape, Newton realized he was visualizing his answer.

"Leprechauns," he said aloud.

"What about Leprechauns?" Commander Joe asked.

Newton opened his eyes. The immense pressure he felt in his head had suddenly dissipated. "Leprechauns are the world's greatest thieves."

Max nodded, understanding. "They did a pretty good job of stealing Gertrude and Herbert."

After Newton had taken a portal from home to the Merriwart kingdom and another to the heart of Macgillycuddy's Reeks, he informed his light-fingered subjects of his royal wish. The thing about Leprechauns is, they don't waste much time hemming and hawing once they have a job to do. Especially if it's a command coming from their King. He was barely done saying "and please be careful," when three of the Leprechaun nation's master thieves had sprung Lester from jail. They brought the ancient green creature back to the Merriwart kingdom, where he was joyfully reunited with his people and the trees.

Which only left Newton with three things to figure out before going home: what to do with the Leprechaun gold, how to abdicate the throne, and how to help Simon, the Troll. Newton was already bored with being King and desperate to return to his normal life. Surprisingly, he also wondered how his brothers were doing at their tryouts. Were they actually making soccer history?

"So how much treasure should we keep for ourselves? You know, as payment for ruling the kingdom," Max asked.

Ever since Newton could remember, his best friend had bragged that one day he'd be fabulously rich. Newton could tell that Max was hoping the day had come much sooner than anticipated.

"I'm not sure," Newton replied.

"Maybe a couple of billion dollars in gold," Max suggested. "That way we'd never have to worry about money again."

Newton had never done much worrying about money, and didn't feel that taking some of the treasure was such a terrific idea. He couldn't explain why, but keeping the gold would feel like stealing. Sure, he could come up with all kinds of justifications as to why he deserved a share, but none of them sat right.

They had been sifting through the suggestion box for hours, reading the Leprechauns' schemes for dispensing with their ill-gotten treasure, without finding an inspired solution. Leprechauns might be geniuses at thievery, but they were definitely a few leaves short of a full clover in the brains department. Their suggestions were either so short-sighted, downright greedy or just plain stupid that Newton was beginning to worry that he might have to stick around and rule the Leprechauns for a few years after all. One cheeky Leprechaun wrote: *Use all the gold to buy France so that we'll have somewhere to go on vacation for free.* Another wrote: *We could eat the gold. I've heard it's actually very good for a Leprechaun's digestion.*

And those weren't the worst. By far! Newton and his friends had almost emptied the suggestion box and were getting very, very desperate, when Commander Joe sighed. "Well, Pokey, looks like this has been a complete waste of time."

"About as useful as licking a metal pole in forty-below weather," Max offered. "You're going to have to get that brain of yours to come up with a solution. But let's do it tomorrow. I really want to sleep in my own bed tonight."

Ignoring his friends, Newton soldiered on against diminishing hope that he would unearth a golden answer in the pile. The next suggestion was idiotic: *Bury it!*

But as it turned out, he was glad that he didn't give up too easily. For the winner was the very last slip of paper he drew out. As soon as he read it, he knew that he had found his answer. In fact, the suggestion was so brilliant that it solved two problems at once. Printed in neat, almost child-like letters was this poem:

> What if Leprechauns roamed from coast to coast,
> Seeking those who need our gold the most?
> Only by being generous to those in need
> Will we finally be able to undo our awful greed.
> Only once all the treasure is out of our hands,
> Will happiness return to our gloomy lands.

The letter was signed, Micaela H. Malarkey. Newton smiled. He informed Seamus that he wished to address his subjects.

Once again the Leprechaun nation gathered in the courtyard.

"I have found an answer," Newton said. "Would Micaela H. Malarkey please step forward." The announcement resulted in ripples of excitement throughout the crowd. Newton waited, expecting some wise old Leprechaun to part the throng and make his way to the stage. Instead, a girl who looked to be the same age as Newton stepped forward.

"I'm Micaela H. Malarkey," the girl said nervously, crossing and uncrossing her legs like she had to pee.

Even for a Leprechaun, Micaela had exceptionally pointy ears. Her face was grubby and her hands were dirty, her clothes torn and tattered. However, the most exceptional feature (by far) of this elf was her hair, which was a shade of red so bright that it appeared to be on fire. The locks were tangled into dreadlocks, and Newton suspected a brush hadn't ventured into the mess in Micaela's lifetime. He leaned forward and spoke to her.

"Did you write this?" He held out her suggestion slip.

The girl nodded meekly.

"And did anybody give you any help?"

"No," Micaela replied, almost in a whisper. "It was all me."

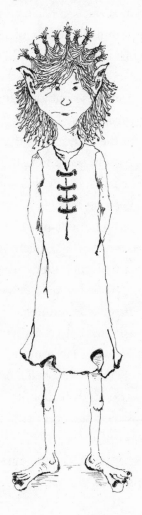

"Well, it's pretty impressive stuff," he said. "Can you please read it out loud for everyone to hear?"

The girl looked like she'd rather do anything but stumble her way through the poem, but she did what he asked. Though her poem was short, Newton could see it had an effect on some of the Leprechauns. They were nodding their heads in agreement.

"So by royal proclamation," said Newton, "I decree that from this day forward, until all illegally obtained gold is fully dispersed, one person from each household shall assist in this duty." Murmurs of disapproval rose from the crowd. Newton knew that no matter how upset they might be at this order, they wouldn't dare go against the King's wishes. Leprechauns had absolute respect for the authority of the monarchy. What else could explain his present position as their ruler?

Newton's next decree would test his subjects' loyalty to the breaking point. "Because Micaela has proven to be wise beyond her years, I hearby remove myself from the kingship and declare her your new ruler. Queen Micaela, will you accept?" The crowd gasped, then went utterly silent.

The poor girl looked so shocked, Newton thought she might pass out. Fortunately she did not.

Before she had a chance to reply, Seamus squeezed himself between the girl and Newton. He coughed dramatically and said to Newton, "Surely there has been a mistake. This child can't be Queen," he sounded disdainful. "She's much too young. Besides, she lives on the other side of the river, close to the forest. I wouldn't be surprised if she had some goblin blood in her." Leprechauns shouted in agreement.

Newton held up his hand dramatically, hoping it showed

far more authority than he felt. "Silence," he demanded. "I need a side meeting."

Newton turned and huddled with Commander Joe and Max. "What do you think?" he asked. "She's pretty young."

"Look who's talking, Pokey," Commander Joe scoffed. "Obviously she has a head on her shoulders and her heart in the right place. Crown her."

Newton turned to Max. "What do you think?"

"Kid power rules," Max said. "And besides, she can't be any worse of a king than you are. No offence, Your Royal Highness."

Newton smiled. His friend was right.

He turned to his subjects. "By the power vested in me, as your King, I hereby abdicate the throne and appoint Micaela H. Malarkey as your new Queen." He paused, trying to come up with something else that sounded official. Instead he added, "What she says, goes." Then Newton took off his crown and placed it on Micaela's head. "I pronounce you Queen Micaela!"

A huge roar came from the crowd. Newton assumed it was a roar of approval.

Though the crown was two sizes too big, Micaela was smiling like she'd just won the lottery. "Thanks, Your Highness."

"Welcome to royalty," Newton said, rather pleased that he had made one little girl quite happy.

When the crowd calmed down, Newton whispered in Michaela's ear. She held up her hand, clearly already getting the hang of being royal. "My first act as Queen is to deal with our mistreatment of Simon, the Troll."

After the official forms had been signed, all that was left for Newton, Max and Commander Joe to do before they left the mountains was to visit Simon. The Troll was still busy at his furnace making safes, because no one had told him to stop. Newton had also brought six Leprechauns with him who were weighed down with supplies and gold bars.

Simon was incredulous that Newton had returned. "Honestly, I never thought I'd see you again," Simon admitted. "I thought the Leprechauns would lock you away until you rotted."

"We got lucky," Newton admitted.

"I'd say it would take a bit more than luck," Simon replied, and demanded to hear the entire adventure.

Though Newton was in a hurry to get home, he, Max and Commander Joe enjoyed retelling the story, even if they may have embellished some of the details slightly. When they came to the end, Newton informed Simon of the reason for his visit.

"While I was still King, I ordered the Leprechauns to pay you for your years of service."

"You did?" Simon said. "How much?"

Newton leaned over and whispered the amount in his ear.

"Well, colour me green!" Simon said, his lifeless eyes blinking in disbelief. "I'm rich beyond rich!"

"You deserve it," Max added.

"There's one more thing," Newton said. "My last order as King was to take you away from here and reunite you with other Trolls. These Leprechauns will guide you wherever you want to go. Just tell them what direction."

Simon gasped and buried his face in his soot-stained hands. Grimy tears squeezed between his fingers and fell to the ground. After a couple of minutes of sobbing he held out his arms. "Come here, Newton. Give me a hug!"

Simon hadn't hugged anyone in decades, so let's just say he was more than a little overexuberant in his display of affection. Smothered in Simon's chest, being squeezed for dear life, trying to gulp down a lungful of air, Newton felt pleased about his decision to make one lonely Troll extremely happy.

"You're welcome," he rasped.

Minutes after leaving Simon and the Leprechauns, Newton, Max and Commander Joe were in Witch Hazel's front yard, staring at the charred remains of her house. As they looked at the wreckage, it finally sank in that Witch Hazel was dead. Newton had never really allowed himself to believe that she was gone. He had always thought that witches, like cats, had more than one life to play with. Knowing he was responsible for her demise made him feel even worse.

"This sucks," Max said. "I feel like crying."

"Me too," said Newton.

"Don't hold back the tears, son," Commander Joe ordered. "I'd be bawling like a bride if I wasn't made of plastic."

Newton put his arm around Max. "Yeah, this does suck. Big time. I miss her already."

As they stood there, the most enchanting woman Newton had ever seen approached. Aside from the fact that she didn't have wings, the woman looked like an angel. A vision of pure beauty. Newton couldn't stop staring at her.

"How are you doing?" she asked.

"Who us?" Newton replied, suddenly feeling self-conscious about his appearance. Like he wished he could go home and shower and change. The more Newton stared at this goddess, the more she seemed familiar. Yet no matter how hard he tried, he couldn't place the face.

"You don't recognize me, Newton, do you," the woman said.

"I'm sorry. No."

A look of annoyance crossed her face. "Just as I suspected. I feel so . . . what's the word I'm looking for . . ."

"*Beautiful, stunning, gorgeous,*" Max said dreamily. He was in a complete stupor.

"Argh! Just as I feared. Am I honestly pretty?"

"Positively goddess-like," Max cooed. "My name is Max."

The woman started scratching at her face as if trying to rip off the skin. "I *know* who you are."

"You do?" Max beamed. "Then you've obviously heard about my acts of bravery."

"Oh dear, I can see saving the world has gone to your head," the woman muttered. She stuck a finger in her ear and began digging earnestly. "Why, oh why, did they do this to me?" she wailed. "I used to be so perfectly ugly that I could make flowers wilt just by a glance. Now this?" She pointed to Max's rapturous face. "Look at the reaction. It's enough to make me become a hermit."

Recognition tickled Newton's brain. "Witch Hazel?" he asked uncertainly. The idea was so preposterous that he felt foolish for even vocalizing it.

Max laughed. "If this enchantress is Hazel, then I'm a wart-infested amphibian."

"That's it!" the woman declared angrily. She picked up a handful of wet earth, pointed a finger at Max and chanted, *"Breath of air and piece of bog, turn this lovesick cretin into a frog!"*

The spell worked perfectly. Max turned from kid to croaker faster than you could say *"Ribbet."* He hopped on the witch's shoes and began licking her leg.

"It's true, Newton. Hazel has lost her ugly. This is the new me in all my awful beauty."

Newton stared at her for a few moments, still not sure that the apparition before him was Hazel. "Wow, what happened?" he asked in amazement, not to mention relief. "How did you escape the fire?"

"I didn't. Not entirely," Hazel replied. "The flames were too much. There was no way I was getting out without being toasted. Fortunately, it was my turn to host our local coven of witches' Fright Night. Unfortunately, that old hag Belinda got to me first. She's always hated my guts. And vice versa. I could have been so spectacularly ugly. Imagine. Most of my body was severely burned. The jealousy it would have inspired! So what does Belinda do?"

Witch Hazel paused so that Newton was forced to ask, "What?"

"She 'mistakenly' put a restorative spell on me. Of course she pretended she didn't mean to but everyone knows you don't 'accidentally' go from being the ugliest witch to this!" Hazel spat.

"So why don't you just change back?"

Hazel started bawling. Loud sobs. Waterworks. In grief

she actually looked even more beautiful. Max the frog started hopping up and down excitedly, flicking his tongue, expertly catching her tears.

"That's the thing about restorative spells—you *can't* undo them, no matter how hard you try. So this is it. For the next few decades, I'm forced to look like some sort of beauty queen. It's horrible!"

Newton felt responsible for her unhappiness. After all, the Leprechauns had burned down her house because of him. "Is there anything I can do?" he asked.

"No," Hazel sniffled. "I suppose I'll just have to get used to it. They say that beauty is only skin deep. But this feels like it's seeped down into my soul."

In spite of Hazel's theatrics, Newton suspected that part of her was putting on a show, that she might not be quite as distraught as she appeared. At the risk of being turned into a cricket, he didn't dare voice this opinion.

Hazel looked up at the sky. "It's going to be a perfect day. I've got to get going. Prime suntanning hours. You understand."

Newton didn't.

"I'm going to rub oil all over my face and expose it to so much sun that my skin will erupt in blisters," she said. "I know it's only temporary, but I've got to up the ugly some-how."

As she hopped on her broom, apparently ready to leave, Newton was alarmed. "What about Max? You can't leave him like that."

"Who says? He made fun of me. Called me beautiful. I think he may even have fallen in love. Where are his manners?"

"Still . . ."

Hazel sighed deeply. "Okay. I'll turn him back. But if he keeps drooling, I can't be responsible for my behaviour." With a wave of her wand, Hazel restored Max to his former self.

Newton realized that Max's affection for Hazel hadn't diminished one iota—he still had a bad case of googly eyes. Before his friend could get a word out, Newton clamped his hand over Max's mouth. "Well, I'd better get Max home. I think he's suffering a bit of sunstroke himself."

Max desperately tried to dislodge Newton's hand.

"I'm still living in the basement," said Witch Hazel. "It survived the fire. In fact, that's the only good thing to come out of all of this. A smaller space is so much easier to keep filthy. Come by and I'll make you some newt-toenail soup," she said, and hopped on her broom. She was about to take off, but paused. "You did good, Newton. Michael and Molly were far more dangerous than any of us guessed."

"Thanks," Newton replied, feeling pleased.

"Well, this is it, I suppose—the official end of the adventure," Max sighed. He stood in his front porch, ready to go into his house.

"Looks that way," Newton said. "Unless of course you get abducted by aliens at your front door."

Max remarked that after everything that had happened, an alien abduction didn't seem impossible. "Do you think you're going to get in trouble from your parents? After all, you did miss the quadruplets' soccer tryouts."

Newton shrugged. "Probably. But a lot less trouble if my brothers made the team. Whatever punishment my mom and dad decide, I wouldn't change a thing. We did what we had to do. What about your parents? Will they be mad?"

"Somehow, I don't think so. They're always pushing me to be a little more adventurous. Besides, I bet they'll be so relieved that I'm safe, they might even forget to be mad." Max held out his hand and they shook. "Thanks for taking me on the adventure. I really had a great time."

"Me too. I've got to admit, you surprised me, Max. You're a much braver person than I ever suspected."

"To tell you the truth, I'm a much braver person than I ever suspected." Max paused. "So what are we going to do tomorrow?"

"Well, if I'm not grounded, we could always start working on my next invention."

"You mean the one that's so top-secret you wouldn't let Seamus say it out loud?"

"That's the one," Newton said. "The schematic drawings survived."

"Are you sure an invisibility machine is a good idea?"

Newton was shocked. "How'd you know I was inventing an invisibility machine? Only Seamus saw the piece of paper."

"You didn't know I had mind-reading abilities?" Max said mischievously.

As possibly the world's most curious boy, Newton hated to be left in the dark about anything. "Come on, how did you find out?"

Max smiled. "I'll never tell." And with that he turned and went inside.

The old Max would never have been able to keep a secret. Newton was impressed.

When Newton arrived home he saw a huge banner hanging from the front porch, congratulating his brothers for making the national team. It seemed like half the town had showed up at his house to celebrate. People were everywhere, and it took Newton twenty minutes to find his family. They were all out in the backyard. His brothers lounged in the pool on floating chairs, wearing sunglasses, being interviewed by a pack of journalists all vying to get their attention. TV cameras and microphones were lined up on the deck. One intrepid reporter went so far as to jump in the pool—clothes and all—to gain a more advantageous spot from which to ask questions. Newton's parents sat on the diving board, proudly watching all of this unfold.

Newton walked up to them. "Congratulations," he said. "They must have played well."

"Oh, Newton," his mother gushed, her eyes glistening with joy. "They're getting their own orange juice commercial! Your brothers are going to be world famous!"

"I shot eighteen hours of video. I didn't miss a single header, corner kick or high-five. It's awesome footage," his father proclaimed joyfully. "We're going to watch it tonight."

"That's fantastic," Newton replied, trying to sound more enthusiastic than he felt.

His father's face suddenly went stern. In spite of the

quadruplets' success, he'd just remembered that he was mad at Newton. "Come over here, we need to talk."

Newton followed his father to the oak tree.

"What happened to the house? When we got back, dishes were broken, there were holes in the ceiling and the hallway. Fortunately the trophy room remain unscathed."

With all that he had been through, Newton had completely forgotten about Lester's panicked path of destruction. His first instinct was to tell the truth. However, he knew that his father would never believe that the damage was caused by a giant from the Kingdom of the Merriwarts. No amount of explaining would change his mind.

Newton decided on a different tack. "I'm sorry. It was stupid, I know. But I was . . . practising soccer."

"Indoors?"

"I didn't want to embarrass myself. Embarrass the family. You know I'm not very good at it. What would the neighbours say if they saw a Wiggins who was less than championship calibre." Newton continued to lie, wondering if he was digging himself a bigger hole.

His father looked confused. "Soccer? Since when are you playing soccer, much less practising? I thought you hated sports."

Next Newton unleashed the biggest whopper of his life. "No. Not at all. That was just an excuse to hide the fact that I'll never be as good as my brothers." He tried to sound really sorry for himself. "Do you know how hard it is living in the shadow of greatness?"

Newton was sure his father would call his bluff, but instead he detected a look of sympathy.

"I can only imagine. But it must be pretty cool as well, knowing you're sharing the same breakfast table with legends. Huh?"

"Yeah, it is, for sure," Newton replied, not daring to make eye contact, fearing he might burst out laughing.

His father raised an eyebrow. "So, did you end up saving the world? I mean, that was the reason you didn't come with us to the soccer tryouts, wasn't it?"

Newton took a deep breath. "Well, to tell you the truth, I sort of lied about that." Trying to convince his father that he had the Right Stuff as a world-saver would be impossible. Why bother?

"Just as I suspected," his father said. "So why didn't you come?"

Newton again decided to speak the only language his father seemed to understand: athletics. "Dad, let me ask you a question. Do you have any sports superstitions?"

His father thought about it for a few seconds. "Well, I never wore clean underwear on game days."

"You didn't?"

When he was a kid, his father explained, he once forgot to change his underwear before a baseball game. "Of course I didn't realize it until I was warming up. And you probably didn't know this about me, but I've always been a person that likes very, very clean underwear. When I realized my oversight, I panicked."

"So what happened? Did you go home?"

"No, I went out and pitched the perfect game. And to be honest, I was never that sensational as a pitcher. So, doing some reverse logic, I realized that the only thing different was the underwear. From that day forward, whenever I played, I played dirty—so to speak. Why do you ask, anyway?"

"Well, I'm a pretty superstitious person and I was convinced that if I came to the tryouts, the quadruplets wouldn't make the team."

"That's nonsense. Are you suggesting that you'd bring bad luck to them?"

"I knew I would."

"But why?"

"I stepped on three sidewalk cracks, walked under a ladder and mistakenly opened an umbrella inside, *all on the same day!*"

His father rubbed his chin. "Let's not forget you were born on Friday the thirteenth as well."

"Actually, my birthday is on the fourteenth."

"Are you sure?"

"Positive."

"Still, that's a whole heap of bad luck. But why didn't you say something?"

"Are you kidding? Even mentioning my superstition might make it come true. I couldn't take that risk. I *wouldn't* take that risk," Newton added dramatically.

"It must have killed you to miss the tryouts."

Newton looked at his father solemnly. "A Wiggins does what a Wiggins needs to do. I had no choice. I knew I needed to take one for the team."

His father, in a rush of emotion, grabbed Newton and hugged him fiercely. "I love you, son. You're good people."

Engulfed in the embrace, Newton felt like a little boy again. He felt safe. He wished his father would never let go.

* * *

When Newton finally crawled into bed he was exhausted. He wasn't sure which had made him more tired—the adventure, or watching hours of mind-numbingly boring footage from the soccer tryouts.

Commander Joe, perched up on the shelf above Newton's bed, peered over the ledge at him. "How you feeling, Pokey?"

"Considering everything we went through, remarkably good. How about you?"

"Well, aside from the War of the Wilted Dandelions in '87, this might have been my most exciting adventure yet. I had a wonderful time."

"Me too," Newton replied sleepily. In the comfort of his bed, he began to appreciate fully the fact that he was still alive. He made a decision to avoid all life-threatening situations for at least the next little while.

Newton must have fallen asleep, when he felt an annoying pinching sensation at the tip of his nose.

"Wake up, Pokey," Commander Joe hissed. "Something's not sitting well with me."

"Couldn't it wait until morning?" Newton said groggily.

"There's something moving in your knapsack."

Newton raised himself up and looked over at his knapsack, which was on the floor beside his desk. Sure enough, it appeared to be alive—like an alien was inside, poking a stick around and trying to get out.

"Should we shoot it?" Commander Joe asked.

"I only have a cap gun," Newton replied, now fully alert.

"What do you think it is?"

Commander Joe said he had no idea.

Just then the knapsack cawed. It wasn't a scary caw, but a sad one. The caw sounded lost.

Newton got out of bed and approached the bag.

"I'd be careful if I were you, Pokey," said Joe.

Delicately Newton unbuckled the top of his knapsack, then quickly stepped back. Maybe there was a rabid animal inside. For a moment nothing moved, and Newton wondered whether he had imagined the whole thing. Just as he was about to reach inside the bag, a beak emerged. And not just any beak—a beak belonging to what turned out to be a pterodactyl! Newton was incredulous. He had forgotten about the egg. How had it not broken?

The bird was no bigger than a soccer ball, but you could see that it wouldn't be long before it was prehistorically huge. The creature started pecking at the ground like a robin looking for worms. Obviously it was hungry.

"What do you think it eats?" Newton asked.

"Hopefully not plastic toys," Commander Joe replied, scurrying up Newton's shirt and into his pocket for safety. "You always said you wanted an unusual pet."

"And it looks like I got one." Newton bent down, picked up the bird and smiled. "I never in a million years thought I'd own my own pterodactyl. It's pretty cool, don't you think, Commander Joe?"

"It sure is, Pokey. It sure is."

Newton and the Time Machine is printed on Ancient Forest Friendly paper, made with 100% post-consumer waste.